GOLDEN SHEAVES, BLACK HORSES

This part of England is not only renowned for the beauty of the countryside but for the quality of its characters.

So I seem compelled to hark back to the time when the village parson kept a cow and a horse in his orchard, and the smell of the good earth and stable had not been polluted by diesel fumes. . . .

Golden Sheaves, Black Horses

Fred Archer

CORONET BOOKS
Hodder and Stoughton

Copyright © 1974 Fred Archer

First published in Great Britain 1974 by
Hodder and Stoughton Limited

Coronet Edition 1976

———————————————————————

Printed and bound in Great Britain for
Coronet Books, Hodder and Stoughton, London,
by Hazell Watson & Viney Ltd,
Aylesbury, Bucks

SBN 0 340 20789 2

AUTHOR'S PREFACE

THIS book about a part of England so aptly described by John Moore as "The Middle West" concerns life in these villages from 1880 until the end of the century. It's a fascinating era, a time when even the grass on the well-trodden footpaths seemed greener.

The characters have fictitious names, but everything recorded happened although sometimes changed slightly in presentation.

This part of England is not only renowned for the beauty of the countryside but for the quality of its characters.

So I seem compelled to hark back to the time when the village parson kept a cow and a horse in his orchard, and the smell of the good earth and stable had not been polluted by diesel fumes. Peewits still follow the plough, the land remains. I have tried to recapture simple things and am proud to live so near to where the village men dug Alf Rogers' smallholding one Sunday. "Come wind come weather, life went on" a life of contrast: the smell of wallflowers and plum blossom, choir outings, the tempest which cost Garnet his life. What the solitary man quoted to Rev Frances Kilvert I pass on to you:

> A little health,
> A little wealth,
> A little house and freedom.
> And at the end
> A little friend
> And little cause to need him.

FRED ARCHER

January 1974

CONTENTS

I

On Netherstone Hill

IT WAS A BLEAK MORNING IN MARCH, 1880. THE brothers Nailus and Garnet Bullin were working at their separate jobs on Netherstone Hill.

Nailus walked the shallow furrow over the limestone, ploughing with his two-horse team. Garnet in the same walled-in field was making his last hurdled pen for the yearling sheep, folded on the swede turnips; in fact Garnet had spent the Winter on the hill making a fresh pen every day for the fattening sheep.

The wind that morning was cutting like a knife, the crowbar which Garnet used to drive in the stakes and let the feet of the hurdles into the stony ground was icy. Not so bad as it had been in January when the iron froze to his hands, but Spring was on the way and this would be Garnet's sixty-sixth and Nailus's sixty-first.

"Whoa," shouted Nailus to Captain and Colonel, his two black shire horses, standing on the head-land with their backs to the wind.

Nailus patted their rounded rumps where the thick hair lay like rugs, black and shiny. This covering had been a barrier to wind, rain, snow and hail as the horses ploughed by day and lay under the burra or shelter of the fir coppice by night.

Garnet walked along the head-land with a sense of purpose, bent under his sacking cape. Little puffs of smoke from his clay pipe were lost in the strong wind.

"Wild weather, Nailus buoy. The fir trees be amust bent like bows this morning." As Garnet spoke to his brother, he tightened his red spotted muffler around his neck and pulled his broad brimmed wide-a-wake hat down on his ears.

Nailus held the plough tails or handles again after he had adjusted the harness on Captain.

"Oi, Garnet, it ketches holt of my ears this morning."

" 'Tis a heast wind and hark how the poplar trees squeals as they rubs together in the coppice."

Garnet spat and took his pipe, douted by the wind, from between his lips, showing two or three teeth like fangs stained with twist tobacco, matching his whiskers.

Garnet leant on his crook and stood with his back under the limestone wall.

"Nothing grows," he said, "and look ya how brown the grass looks over the wall."

" 'Never come March, never come Winter' our old Dad was used to say, dost remember you?" Nailus replied. "And another thing, what bist worrying about, Garnet, cus as soon as they ship a finished the roots yonder, they ull be hung up in a butcher's shop."

Garnet slipped his clay pipe under the leather york or strap below his left knee and cleared his throat. "I be up yer all weather, unt I? If it snows the ship got to be fed, but the gaffer won't let thee plough snow into the ground, it's s'pposed to kip the ground cold else."

Nailus looked towards his brother with the far away look so common to followers of the plough. He screwed his eyes against the wind, the wind which rippled the brown wiry grass in the next field like tiny waves on a pond. Here the outlying bullocks wrapped their tongues around tufts of this coarse herbage and fed.

The peewits were still in flocks as they had been all the Winter, foraging for food amongst the flat stones and flat cakes of bullock dung. Their plaintive cry when they flew high above the hill chilled the March air, then as the weak watery sun stood like an amber ball behind the clouds—clouds that chased each other only to be lost behind the sky line—a lark ventured up from the brown sward and twittered its song, motionless apart from the flutter of its outstretched wings.

"Well, Garnet," Nailus said, "I suppose thee hast bin up yer all Winter along with them farting sheep, squat on a hurdle blowing yer bacca. How about the fire further along under the wall?" Garnet looked towards the blue smoke from the burning gorse and walked towards it.

"We ull now have our bait [lunch], Nailus buoy. The kettle's on the buyle, but ull them two dumb animals a thine run away if they are left?"

"Run away," laughed Nailus. "Gunpowder udn't shift them cratures! It's time past our gaffer Tom Samson sent um to market and bought me some tolerable hoss flesh."

The brothers stood near the fire and Garnet poured two mugs of tea out of the iron kettle. Nailus uncorked a beer bottle, tipped a little milk he had brought from the dairy into each mug, turning the brown brew to a soft grey colour, and put the bottle back into the frail basket where it came from.

"What surprises do you recon we a got in our frail baskets this morning?" Garnet said, as he undid the knots in the red and white kerchief.

"Oi, bread and cheese and an onion, that's the usual, unt it?" and Nailus added, "It's is to be hoped that the cheese unt as hard as it was yesterday. I had to cut mine with the coulter as runs in front of the share on the plough."

Garnet munched his lunch, throwing the rind of his cheese to Rosie his sheep dog who lay quietly under the wall on a corn sack. Every time Garnet offered her the rind she pricked up her shaggy ears, opened her mouth just wide enough and caught the rind like a child catching a ball.

Rosie was a cross between a collie and an Old English bob-tailed sheep dog; she was hardy, sensible as a Christian, a good sheep dog but also had what was known as a good nose. She would find a rabbit for Garnet if it lay in the rubble which formed the middle of the tidy dry stone wall of Netherstone

Hill. She would whine and paw at the stones while Garnet levered a hole in the wall with his hurdle bar, flat on the side for driving stakes in the ground; Garnet would ferret with his hand until his fingers detected the soft fur of a rabbit's tail, then sliding his hand in further underneath he grasped the hind legs and out came another meat portion for Garnet and Jane Bullins' dinner.

Nailus was thinking of the long Winter weather still chilling his blood when he noticed the partridges had broken up from their coveys or flocks and paired and were mating. The persistent click of their metallic call could be heard quite plainly, carried by the wind from the banks and hollows of the hill, which was entrenched like a camp, affording easy cover from wind and weather.

A puff of smoke and steam came from Netherstone Station. The ten-thirty was on her way on the branch line, the long chimney stack of the engine standing out plain behind the short cropped hedges of the track.

Nailus pulled out his great turnip watch from his cord waistcoat pocket. "Yonder, Garnet. Steam from the iron road. That's the ha' past ten, unt it, and her's to time aguan," he said, looking at the hands of his watch in wonder.

Garnet took up his crook from against the wall, called Rosie and turning to Nailus answered, "Oi, 'tis the bait time train and I got work to do. Bist a gowain to tighten the hosses' traces again? I got a feeling as Master Samson ull be up on the hill presently."

Nailus shouldered his frail basket, put the dead root of an elder bush on the fire to keep it in until dinner time, and slouched towards his team.

He slouched because that was how he walked as he held the plough day after day, bent to form almost a part of the implement. Where Garnet was fat, squat and red faced, Nailus was tall, lean, angular.

"Kyup, Colonel, Kyup, Captain," Nailus told his two horses.

The pair pricked up their ears, turning slowly, pulling the plough along the head-land.

Nailus tipped his plough to the right so that the sheel board or mould board scraped a shallow mark on the unploughed head-land, then pulling hard on his right rope rein guided his horses so that Captain stood in the open furrow. "Hard mouthed old fellow thee bist," he thought and at a click of his tongue the team plodded on. The harness jingled, a plough wheel squeaked, and apart from the occasional snort from the horses' steaming nostrils and the grinding of limestone as it was turned up by the ploughshare, there was no sound but the wind blowing the trees in the coppice. The soil was light and fell in crumbling furrows, so unlike the clay of the vale where the yellow, putty-like earth stood up in rows behind the plough like rashers of bacon, unworkable without a frost.

Tom Samson rode breeched and gaitered on his weight-carrying hunter towards the bridle gate, opened the spring latch with his stick and went towards his carter Nailus. Trotting along the head-land he waited astride his horse until Captain and Colonel pulled the plough to the end of the furrow.

"Marning, Gaffer," Nailus said, "Keenish wind, unt it?"

"Ay, I suppose it is bleak up here," Tom replied. Then looking at the furrows he said, "Turn the team back again, Nailus, and go a few yards and then stop."

"Cumming back," called Nailus, and the pair of shires turned back into the other furrow.

"Whoa," shouted the farmer, then said to Nailus, "Just put the land wheel a bit deeper." (The small wheel on the left.)

Nailus took his iron spanner from the staple on the plough tails and pushed the pointed end into the hole in the set screw which kept the iron collar tight against the stem of the wheel. Before slackening the screw he marked the wheel stem. The upright part connected to the axle with a stone which he used as a school teacher would use a piece of chalk. When the screw was slack the wheel rose about half an inch. Nailus tightened it and on the stem exposed a cream line where the collar held the wheel stem before.

"That's better," Tom Samson said. "You weren't hardly deep enough before."

"That's quite right, Gaffer," Nailus replied, "But do get me two better young hosses and I'll go deeper still."

Tom Samson rode away. The horses jibbed and snatched. Nailus swore about horses and farmers, stopped the ploughing and put the furrow wheel back where it was before. The ploughing went well and the horses were not being mauled and overworked.

Funny thing, he thought, how farmers always want their ploughmen to do the impossible and plough into the stone on Netherstone Hill. Then Nailus muttered to himself as the horses stepped along together, "It's a pair of young horses I want." Scarcely had the words been said when he thought again, "If the gaffer buys three-year-olds, I'm sixty-one and they will be lissom. Perhaps they will plough too fast for my old legs."

"Hark ya," shouted Garnet over the wall as Nailus turned once more on the head-land.

Nailus called "whoa" and once more his team stood together, but this time they laid their ears, looked round at the carter and showed the whites of their sleepy eyes.

"Thank ya, Garnet. I can year the horn, 'tis the hounds a breaking cover from yonder wood." With these words Nailus grabbed the coupling stick hooked to Captain and Colonel's bits and patting them both on the neck, said in a quiet voice. "Whoa, my buoys, it's only the hunt. You've seen and heard it times before to-day."

Garnet looked into the wind and spotted some men in hunting pink around the wood. "He ull like enough come this road," he said. "Foxes run with the wind, must be very nigh the last meet."

"And if it's the old stager in front of the pack," said Nailus, "He ull come into coppice up yer." He had no sooner spoken than the sound of hounds leaving the cover made Captain and Colonel potter about on the head-land, then between the two men, the old dog fox ran, the following wind blowing into his outstretched brush as he ran with ease half a mile in front of the pack into the coppice.

"Yonder," Nailus shouted. "He's gone to ground among the elder bushes."

The pack ran across Nailus's ploughing and Garnet's sheep packed themselves tightly against the hurdle fence.

The huntsman in pink with white breeches galloped over the ploughed furrows calling to Nailus, "Have you seen the fox?"

"Oi," Nailus replied, "he's down in the Big Earth."

"Gone to ground" the huntsman blew on his horn as the hounds whimpered and whined in the coppice. The first whipper-in rode up the hill, his horse foaming from mouth and mane.

"Is the earth a deep one, Carter?" the huntsman said.

"Devilish deep, unt it, Garnet, and solid rock. The badgers lies in there sometimes, and if I was in thy place I udn't risk putting terriers down there."

The other men in pink arrived, then the side-saddled ladies, veiled and bowler-hatted.

The tweed of the farmers' jackets was such a contrast as they sat astride their strong cobs.

"Morning, Reverend," Garnet and Nailus said as Rev Robert Cuthbert, Vicar of Netherstone, passed. "Good morning, men," he replied. "I gather Master Reynard has gone to ground."

"'Fraid so," Nailus said. "Wily he is, you know. I'll warrant he's seven foot down in the ground."

The huntsman called the pack away from the earth where the fox had gone to ground and with the plaintive note of the hunting horn sounding over the hill, the followers moved away following the liver and white and tan hounds towards the next wood.

"Captain, Colonel, Cup Cup," Nailus said and like a small

boat on a brown sea, the plough ripped another furrow, the peewits dipped and dived like seagulls. The larks and hawks viewed the scene from above.

When the brothers had eaten their midday meal by the burning wood fire under the wall, the afternoon went by till Garnet saw his sheep safely folded and fed and went down the hill to his cottage. Nailus rode sidesaddle on Captain and Colonel followed. The jingle of harness, the sweat marks dried white in the wind, made patterns of trace harness on the horses' backs.

Aaron Hicks, gamekeeper to Squire Mathison, stood camouflaged under a March naked oak tree, fingers ready for the trigger of his gun, waiting for the hawks and carrion crows which would in a few weeks be a pest to his broody hen reared pheasants cooped in the nearby meadow.

"Good night to tha, Aaron. What time dost thee finish work you?" Captain stumbled over the stony track as Nailus said his evening piece to the keeper.

Aaron walked towards Captain and grabbing his mullen [bridle] shouted, "Whoa." He then asked Nailus if he had seen Sep Sands on the hill. Nailus looked hard at the keeper and at his gun and spaniel dog.

"Sep? Why, that bastard son of our gaffer's he ull soon be on his road to the Cider Mill pub." Aaron turned and looked down the hill towards the Cider Mill.

"Yes," he said, "I know he's Master Samson's bastard, and his mother Mary has been dead for five years or more, but he's a waster, a rodney, I wish to God I could catch him poaching this hill."

"What's the latest, have he bin round your traps and wires?" asked Nailus.

Aaron drew closer to the carter mounted on Captain and said quietly, "He poached about fifty rabbits out of my snares last night, leaving the traps with their jaws sprung too, and the wires with the slip knot tight and fur everywhere."

Nailus looked down at him and exclaimed, "He's crooked,

dost know and a bragger. I'll listen to his boasting in the pub tonight. Ah, it yunt right for Squire Mathison to be robbed by a work-shy sod. How many did he leave you, Aaron? None, I'll warrant."

2

The Cider Mill

JOE BADGER AND HIS WIFE MARY KEPT THE BLACK
and white thatched pub known as 'The Cider Mill', at the top of
a winding lane which led to Netherstone Hill.

The roof was made of straw thatch, but sparrows, starlings
and other birds of the garden had tunnelled holes in it and the
winds of winter had blown wisps of straw into the orchard of
knarled apple trees.

The sparrows for years now had nested in the roof, emerald
green moss covered some of the barer parts, making the house
seem like just another fold in the hill itself.

When the wind was fresh the Inn sign swung to and fro on its
hinges so that it squeaked like a whimpering puppy. This painted
board, the work of a local artist, showed passers-by a scene of
cider-making in the Orchard; the great black horse with the
harness of his collar hitched to the wooden pole stood waiting
on the outside of the circular stone trough. The wooden gearing
on the pole was fixed to the cheese-like stone upright in the
trough. In front of the mill stone the artist had painted heaps of
rosy red apples and behind the tan coloured crushed pomace or
pulp a little boy dressed in a drab coat, corduroy breeches torn
at one knee, a conical shaped hat and red muffler stood at the
horse's head with one hand on the rein of the bridle.

Inside the pub kitchen, the regular farm men of Netherstone
sat on the semicircle of the settle in front of the fire talking the
evening away about sheep, cows, horses, foxes, cider and
servant girls.

Sep Sands the poacher was usually first customer at the Cider

Mill. It was more than he dare do to sit on the settle, being a mere twenty-two years old and the bastard son of Tom Samson; he crouched in the inglenook on a narrow seat below where Joe smoked his bacon in the wide chimney near the salt box.

Tom Samson had paid for Sep to go to school so that Sep could read and write and his talk was much less broad than that of the farm men.

It was to the Cider Mill that the dealers from the nearest town came and bought rabbits and game from this unrepentant poacher. Here in the chimney corner lay the corn sack full of his poached fur and feathers, and his mongrel dog stretched out on the sack laid his ears if a stranger came near.

Sep had sneaked across the orchard on an evening when the dealers were coming to the Cider Mill. He came as sly as a brandy smuggler, sat down in the chimney corner and read racing news from the local paper. Mary Badger, the landlord's wife, filled Sep's pewter pot with beer from the trammed barrel in the drink house.

Joe Badger looked hard at Sep, then at the sack of the poached rabbits and game and said, "You been at it again, boy."

Sep laughed, looked up from the paper and replied, "Yes, I've got to live and make a few shillings to pay Widow Prew for my lodgings and then I must have a dabble on the horses. I see the Major is running that useful horse of his at Oatfield Point-to-Point." Sep put his hand in his pocket and jingling his money brought out a shilling. "Put this on for me, will you, Joe, I see the Major's horse is priced at 5 to 1."

Soon the sound of hob-nailed boots was heard on the cobbled path. It was Nailus and Garnet Bullin coming for their supper cider. Garnet held his dog Rosie by a chain. Rosie didn't like the mongrel in the inglenook so Garnet chained her to the table leg.

"Good evening, men," Joe said as his two customers sat on the settle. "Your usual, I expect."

"Oi, a drap a cider to slake our thirst," said Nailus.

Joe brought two crock mugs full, cold from the drink house and the brothers drank with a few sighs and Ah's.

Mary Badger sat in a chair by the fire knitting, then raising her eyes she looked at the brothers and said, "You two chaps are very quiet tonight."

Garnet looked into the fire, then turning to his brother said, "Thee tell her, Nailus, you saw Aaron tonight."

Nailus took another sip of cider, blew his nose and looked towards Sep.

"That's the gentleman as plagues good honest folk in Netherstone poaching rabbits from Aaron's traps and wires." He poked his ash stick towards the sack at Sep's feet and the mongrel dog snarled showing a set of white teeth.

"That's where Squire Mathison's rabbits be, in that sack, Mary."

Then Garnet raised his voice. "The truth needs no study. Sep poaches regular like and he was before the Beaks at Oathill the other week."

"Five shillings they fined him and in our old chap's young days he ud a been transported. Our old chap," Nailus muttered. "He lies near the tower in the churchyard."

Sep looked at the two work-weary men who looked after Mr Samson's sheep and horses, Mr Samson who had fathered him. Secretly he admired their honesty, their faithfulness to their master, but he wasn't going to be shown up in Badger's pub by them.

"Look here," he said, "you say that rabbits from Aaron Hicks' traps are in that sack. Just you prove it. Netherstone Hill doesn't all belong to Mathison and just because I don't follow a plough horse's tail week in week out or hurdle farting sheep in pens on turnips all my life, why pick on me? You and your rough cider in crock mugs."

Garnet turned to Mary and Joe Badger who stood by her, and said, "That's education for ya, no respect for their elders, too proud now to drink cider—it's got to be beer and a newspaper to read for him.''

Sep smiled in a cynical way. "Do you two men want a tip for the Point-to-Point meeting? I'm putting a shilling on the Major's horse.''

"Gambling, thurs another vice I'll warrant," Nailus told his brother. "I be mortal proud as thee and me have allus worked for our bread; fearing God and honarying the Queen's my maxim.''

A horse and cart came up the lane. It was the dealers from Oathill. Sep got up from his seat and carried the sack through the door out into the night.

"Good night," said he, as he left the Cider Mill. Nailus and Garnet were silent; they drank up the cider and left for home.

"Can't blame Joe Badger, I suppose," Garnet said to his brother. "But it appears that the Cider Mill harbours Sep in his law breaking. Good night Nailus, I'll see ya in the maorning on the hill.''

3

Shot Guns

TOM SAMSON'S TWO MEN LIVED IN TWO COTTAGES next door to each other, just across the yard from the farmhouse opposite the duck pond. Jane, Garnet's wife, had reared two sons. Both were married: Frank was in the police force, and Harry worked on a farm in the next village.

Kate, Nailus's wife, was childless, she helped Sarah Samson in the farmhouse as charwoman.

The fact that Sep Sands was a thief made Kate collect the hens' eggs twice a day. She locked Mrs Samson's ducks up every night and their dog Rosie lay on the straw in an empty loose box adjoining the stable.

If only Sep could be trusted! It seemed as if he had a continual grudge against Tom Samson for his very existence. It's true that Aaron Hicks was gamekeeper to Squire Mathison, but Tom was the best tenant farmer on the small estate and worried over Sep's poaching and thieving.

The days passed by and Aaron knew that soon his hen pheasants would be sitting on their eggs under the stone walls of the hill or among the briars in the coppices and he would be collecting broody hens to hatch out broods of pheasant chicks in coops and runs in the paddock. If only Sep would work like the other men in the village, he thought.

"Have you seen him this morning?" he asked Nailus as his plough horses turned on the head-land. Nailus knew who the gamekeeper referred to and just nodded an answer adding, "Oi, the young varmint was up on the Knap at fust light and there's no mistaking it was his shot gun as echoed round the hill. Whether it was one of your long taileduns [pheasants] as fell out of the fir tree I can't say, but he picked up something or other.''

Aaron was not surprised, but before walking down the hill with his gun he thanked Nailus. "Don't say anything, I'll catch him one of these maornings.''

Some days after, when the golden glow of what promised to be a beautiful sunrise made the dawn just light enough to show the row of beech trees on the skyline of hills ten miles away, Aaron lay with his gun in the coppice among the blackberry briars near to the Knap. Sep passed, creeping under the wall a few yards away carrying his muzzle-loader gun. He walked alongside a row of trees, fir trees as green as summer and ash trees bare apart from the hanging keys of last year with their seed pods chattering in the early morning breeze.

Sep stopped under an ash and aimed at the topmost bough. A cock pheasant fell to the ground like a stone. It's true the bird was out of season to the gentry, but everything is in season to a poacher who sells game at the pub.

As soon as the powder smoke, black as the night which had just ended, died away, Sep reloaded his gun, ramming the black powder down into the breach. Then the wad was pushed tight with the ramrod and finally a measure of shot and another wad were pressed lightly down from the barrel's end. From his waistcoat pocket he took one firing cap and slipped it under the hammer of the gun, having pulled the hammer back into the cocked position.

"Ay, you thieving swine, drop that gun," shouted Aaron as he approached from his hide. "Drop it, I say," Aaron shouted in a louder voice.

Sep looked first at the red, gold, white and brown plumage of the bird at his feet, then at the gamekeeper.

"You come near to me, Master Hicks, and I'll pepper those tweeds with lead. That's a warning, mind, or my name's not Sep Sands.''

Aaron walked up towards Sep saying "I've got you now—it's a fair capture and don't talk silly about shooting at folk."

Sep levelled his gun pointing it at Aaron, but the gamekeeper took a quick shot at Sep's knee. It was as if the gun and the keeper were one, the gun like a third arm to him. Sep fell to the ground and groaned, dropping his gun and lying in pain beside the dead pheasant.

Aaron took his muffler off and tied it tight around the part of Sep's legs which oozed blood. He carried the young poacher under the wall and gave him a drink of cider from his costrel bottle.

Nailus came up the hill. He had been watching the whole thing from a distance and after tying his horses to a hawthorn tree he ran as fast as his legs would carry him to where the poacher lay.

"Is he hurt bad, Aaron?"

Aaron said, "Well, it's bad enough but I've stopped the bleeding. Did you see what happened?"

Nailus looked at the keeper and poacher, replying "Oi, I should think I did. It was either thee or he as was going to be shot, and like enough if you ud have had the charge from that there blunderbuss of 'is, it ud have blowed yer head off."

As if from nowhere Garnet came carrying a hurdle.

On Netherstone Hill's eastern slopes and on the flat top Garnet and Nailus noticed everything. They were its unofficial guardians. If people came from Oatfield town to gather blackberries or mushrooms they wanted to know who gave them permission.

"We has to work hard for our fittle," Garnet often said, "and we don't like to see our gaffer robbed."

Garnet came nearer with the hurdle, looked at Sep and said, "Looks to me, my buoy, you be a stretcher case."

Aaron held one end of the hurdle and Garnet the other while Nailus took his overcoat off.

Nailus put his overcoat on the hurdle like a blanket and Aaron warned him it might get blood stained.

"Well, it won't be the first time there bin blood on that coat. Our old chap wore it in the Crimea."

The three men carried the wounded poacher down the hill to Tom Samson's house where Sarah the farmer's wife put a clean towel around the wound. Her husband Tom drove his horse and trap to Netherstone Railway Station sending an urgent telegram from there to the doctor at Oatfield.

Meanwhile Nailus was sent for the village policeman.

As he and the policeman walked to the farmhouse, Nailus told the story over and over again that Aaron shot in self defence, always adding, "If he hadn't done, mind ya, Constable, young Sep ud a blowed his 'ead off."

The doctor arrived and found Sep on Samson's sofa sipping brandy as Aaron stood beside him.

"Ah," the doctor said. "We must get those lead shots out of that leg."

So with a dose of laudanum to kill the pain, the doctor who had hastened in his trap from Oatfield and whose horse Garnet rubbed down as it sweated in the stable cleaned the wound, and probed for the shot from Aaron's gun in Sep's leg.

When he had cleaned up the leg Garnet and Nailus took Sep down the road to Widow Prew's house in a wheelbarrow. Here he lay the day through, pillowed and cushioned on her sofa.

The constable sat in Samson's kitchen with Aaron. He asked to see him alone, but Nailus insisted on going in when he returned from Widow Prew's cottage.

"I knows the whole story," he declared. "It a bin brewing up for weeks. Sep have poached our hill and he has got what he deserves."

"Now, Nailus," the constable pleaded, "I've had your story. Please let me have Aaron's. Was it daylight when you shot Sep? You do admit shooting him, I gather." Aaron shifted on the windsor chair, his nailed boots scraping the flagstone floor.

"It was just getting light, the sun hadn't risen," Aaron answered.

Nailus butted in, "What odds is that, Constable?"

The village man in blue with shiny buttons cleared his throat as he replied. "Some crimes are more serious at night, but let Aaron speak." Aaron made his statement and the policeman wrote it down in his book. After Aaron had signed it, he pulled the elastic band around the hard cardboard covers.

"Well, that's pretty clear," he said. "You and the witness say you shot in self defence but you did shoot to wound him, that's true, isn't it?"

A tear trickled down Aaron's cheek and he swabbed it with his kerchief. He sniffed a few times before he spoke, then said, "I've never hurt anybody before but I had to shoot and his leg will mend. I'm sorry now for the young chap, sorry it had to come to this. Shall I be charged?"

"'Fraid so," the constable said, "but under the circumstances I'm sure the bench will be as lenient as they can be."

Soon after a summons was issued against Aaron for shooting at Sep with intent to wound him. Widow Prew and the Oatfield doctor got the poacher on his feet again and bandaged he went to the sessions. Squire Mathison retired from the local bench for the hearing as he was an interested party. The local people of Netherstone went to Oatfield to hear the case.

Tom Samson took Nailus in the horse and trap, and explained to him how important it was not to contradict himself, and only to answer the questions.

Aaron stood in his best tweeds in front of the magistrates. He looked quite calm, knowing full well that Sep was getting better.

Joe Badger from Cider Mill brought Sep to court in his governess cart.

Sep limped into court, nodding to Aaron who stood at the bar. Charges were read out and when Nailus Bullin's name was called as witness, he trembled as he held the Bible and took the oath.

Nailus turned to the bench and said, "There was no need for

me to swear on the Book, I speaks the truth, and the truth needs no study."

The clerk looked with understanding at Nailus, and said, "We don't doubt your word, Mr Bullin, but we must keep to the law."

"Now, Mr Bullin, will you tell the court in your own words just what happened on the morning of the shooting."

"Sep a bin a poaching our hill too long," Nailus replied. Tom Samson looked at his carter and Nailus knew he had started badly.

"Now, Mr Bullin, we don't want to hear that. What did you see that morning?"

"Well, Sir, I was going up the hill with my team, excuse me, I mean Master Samson's team, when I spied Sep creeping towards the ash tree. Now that pheasant as he shot roosted the night afore. The *cock up, cock up*, could be heard on the edge of night. I saw the smoke from his gun, and the bird fall. Then Master Hicks the keeper came out of the thorns and challenged Sep."

"What happened then?" Nailus was asked.

"Ay, they levelled their guns at each other like soldiers, and Aaron got his shot in first."

"Thank you, Mr Bullin, that will be all."

The constable was called and the doctor told of extracting lead shot from Sep Sand's leg. Aaron pleaded guilty, but only to shooting in self defence.

Sep admitted poaching, also to aiming at Aaron. The Chairman addressed Aaron pointing out it was a serious charge to take the law into his own hands and had it not been for the fact that Sands had aimed his gun at him it would have been a case for the assizes.

"However," the Chairman went on, "we cannot deal with the matter lightly, and you will go to prison for one month."

Aaron dropped his head. Nailus blew his nose and looked at Mr Samson.

As the defendant was led away the court cleared silently, but the villagers of Netherstone stood a little while outside the Town Hall of Oatfield, talking amongst themselves, while Sep was helped into Joe Badger's cart to ride home to Widow Prew's cottage.

Garnet said to Nailus that evening in the rick yard:

"Such things that we have witnessed today would never happen if everyone went on with their work comfortable like thee and me."

4

Wilf Cob, Under Keeper

Squire Mathison was faced with an urgent problem while Aaron was away. He had no gamekeeper on his estate. I suppose the relationship between him and Tom Samson was not exactly that of landlord and tenant alone; they were good friends, they shot and hunted together. So the first thing Tom did when he knew that there was no one to look after the game on Netherstone Hill was to go to his landlord.

Squire Mathison had only been married a year. His wife Annette was young and pretty, 25 in fact, with auburn hair; her face had shone in Netherstone the past Winter like another sun. She was the daughter of a stockbroker and had finished her education in France, was a fearless rider to hounds and organist at the church. Her husband's parents had died a couple of years ago, and she was well suited to be the lady of the Manor. She talked to the landworkers, the children, smiled at the roadman after giving him tobacco as he swept the village street.

"Just like one of we, no side on her," Nailus said to Mrs Samson in the yard while Tom Samson talked with the Squire at the Manor. His first question was "How shall you manage without Hicks, Mr Mathison?"

"Funny thing, Tom," the Squire replied, "I have been thinking of getting an under keeper and in fact a lad off my neighbour's estate has applied for a post, but it's a problem, Tom, of finding really good lodgings for him. He's rather a superior boy, and I don't fancy that life in one of my cottages would suit him, and honestly I don't feel like having him here. You know Annette's quite young, a good cook, mind you, and we have a good house-maid. What do you think, Tom?"

Tom said straight away, "He can lodge with us."

"That's fine. You sure that's all right with Sarah? Don't spoil the lad, but you know what cottage life is like."

And so Wilf Cob arrived to take charge of the covers or coverts until Aaron returned, and then to be gamekeeper under him.

Tom Samson sent Nailus with him on his first morning to show him around the hill. Nailus pointed out the fox earths, badger sett and likely places where the pheasants would be sitting. Then past Benedict's Pool at the bottom end of one coppice.

"Yer," said Nailus, "this pool is a mystery."

Wilf looked surprised as he said, "Looks all right to me. There's water-cress, a few mallard and moorhens, and no doubt some coarse fish."

"Ah," Nailus sighed, "that unt all. It's a unkid place, even the hermit as lives with his pig in the Folly won't come past yer at night. He don't care a damn for nobody, man nor beast, but he won't pass the pool at night!"

Wilf looked puzzled and said he had been on another estate and was not afraid of the dark.

"It unt the dark as is to be feared up yer, it's the night of the full moon. Here's where a 'ooman in white walks the footpath and once you have seen her you be never the same again," Nailus went on. "Oi there's many lying in the churchyard as years ago have been frit to death by the white 'ooman."

"Why does this happen, Nailus? It looks so peaceful with the ducks and all that."

Nailus lit his clay pipe, asking Wilf if he would like a smoke. Wilf pulled a packet of cigarettes from his pocket saying, "I use these, thank you."

Nailus puffed the blue smoke from his pipe and leant on the bridle gate.

"The ducks you say, Wilf? Well, they won't be yer when the

moon's full—they fly down to the clay pits. Mind," he added, "this female don't appear regular, her appears when things be amiss in the village. It's as if the One above warns us of our transgressions like."

They passed the pool and went home and Wilf settled in with the Samsons.

The time soon slipped by and Aaron was home again. The past happenings at Netherstone were now like a bad dream to the villagers.

Squire Mathison's gamekeeper Aaron had always had an air of mystery about him; he talked very little about himself, in fact he talked very little about anything. He had been in the village ten years or more, living alone in a cottage adjoining the ash coppice, the pheasant-rearing paddock being on the other side of the garden fence. The only thing Netherstone folk knew about Aaron's past was that he was a widower. No one asked questions. There is no doubt that all the people in Netherstone parish were glad to see Aaron home again. He and Wilf soon were busy with the young pheasants, and as they walked through the rearing paddock the head keeper thought that having a month away had been a blessing, for had not this happened he would have been alone again with the pheasants and the Squire would not have engaged Wilf.

Although Aaron's understudy was just nineteen years old he soon proved his worth. In fact Aaron said to Nailus in Samson's stable that young Wilf had a gift for rearing pheasants and trapping vermin.

"Ah," the old carter replied, "you've either got it in yer or not. 'Tis just the same as hosses. If you handle um quiet like, they ull do everything for ya, bar talk, and I'm a gwain to tell tha you can talk um through gateways avout using reins. Sensible as Christians, hosses be."

As Nailus talked to the keeper Garnet came into the yard carrying an orphan lamb.

"I shall have to see Master Samson and get a drop of milk off the house cow. Well, I myuns the cow as he keeps a purpose to supply the Manor with milk and butter.''

Aaron looked at Garnet as the lamb bleated from under his herden sacking cloak he wore at lambing time.

''The ewe's dead I suppose, Garnet?'' he ventured to say.

Garnet looked hard at the cobbled stone yard and never spoke for a moment—it was as if something caught him in his throat making him swallow several times before words would come, then at last he muttered, ''Oi, liver fluke. I would be worried we lost scores of yows [ewes] last lamb rearing time, I damn near jumped in the moat pond.''

Aaron spoke up straight away, making sure that the old man knew how well his shepherd stood in Tom Samson's eyes at Netherstone farm.

''It's like this, Garnet, I'm a gamekeeper and things often go wrong.'' As Aaron spoke he pointed at his muzzle-loader gun under his arm adding, ''Here's my friend. Now if the hawks, stoats, weasels and such like kill my young pheasants I have to guard them with powder and shot. Mind you, it was hard to shoot at Sep when he was poaching.''

Garnet didn't hesitate. ''Hard? You done right, buoy, he ud a bin sent to Van Deemans land in Fayther's time, transported I myuns.''

''How is Sep?'' Aaron asked.

''Now I don't go out of my way to inquire about the health of the likes of him, but Badger told me at the Cider Mill he's as right as ninepence.'' To this Garnet added his final comment, ''He's a damn sight better than he deserves to be, the idle rodney. But I have some good news. Joe Badger says that he's left Widow Prew's house and got himself a job on the railroad at Oatfield cleaning ingins and recons he ull be a fireman. He is twenty-two, ya know, and damn me at that age I could mow an acre of mowing grass in a day with the dismal [scythe].''

5

Sep Sands Returns

AFTER A FEW MONTHS AT OATFIELD STATION CLEANING railway engines and beginning to learn the job as a fireman Sep got tired of his regular hours. The iron road was so different from the green fields of Netherstone.

When he was off duty it was his custom to walk over to his native village on Sunday nights and drink at Joe Badger's pub. Just before the hunting season got under way, Joe Badger told Sep as he drank his beer in the Cider Mill that Major Forbrooke was looking for a strapper or under groom.

"Oh yes, the Major at the Grange. I backed his horse at the Point-to-Point and won," Sep replied.

Mary Badger laughed at Sep's navy blue railway suit. "Ah," she said, "I recon breeches and gaiters would look better on you, but can you ride?"

"Ride!" Sep answered. "Of course I can ride. I learnt first of all on Samson's pony, then at the school he sent me to. But where am I to live? Widow Prew won't have me back now."

Joe's eyes met Mary's and a silent message seemed to pass from one to the other. A message which when transferred into words resulted in the husband and wife both saying together, "You can lodge here, Sep."

"Well, thank you both," he said. "I haven't got the job yet, but if I do I'll help you in the orchard with the fruit and the pigs, I'm most grateful."

Major Forbrooke kept about a dozen hunters at the Grange besides brood mares. He had some useful brood mares and picked one of the best thoroughbred stallions in the stud book to serve them in the late spring.

His stud groom was an old retainer who had served under him in the Army.

The Major, a retired Cavalry man, was a good judge of horse flesh. The fact that his horse won at the Hunt Point-to-Point was but a minor triumph for Forbrooke stable.

He had bred winners at some of the classic races in the calendar. At fifty-seven, the Major was a joint master of the local hunt.

Sep Sands called at the Grange and applied for the job as under groom.

"Come back in a couple of days, my boy," the Major said. This gave him a chance to inquire in Netherstone of Sep's ability with horses. He already knew of course of the poaching episode, but that didn't worry him very much as long as he could ride, and help to school horses.

Sep returned and met Major Forbrooke, and Lewes, the groom, in the yard.

"Jump on Mettle, the iron grey, lad," the Major ordered, winking at Lewes. Mettle was well named—a headstrong gelding of about five years.

Sep clutched the reins, dug his knees well into Mettle's ribs and cantered round the three-acre field. Turning to Lewes and strutting in the gateway with both hands deep in his breeches pockets, the master of the Grange said, "Damn useful chap I'd say. Got quite a good seat, you know; I've known officers in the Cavalry who didn't sit in the saddle as well as Sands. I'll engage him, to hell with his poaching."

As Sep left the saddle in the field gateway Major Forbrooke shouted, "Good lad, Sands. When can you start?"

"Thank you, Sir," Sep replied. "I'll give notice to the company, I expect it will be a fortnight's time."

"Blasted pity you know, Lewes, for a young country chap to be a grease monkey on the railroad."

Then as the Major turned to Sep, telling him that it wouldn't be all riding horses to exercise. "Oh no, there's the tack to clean, the horses to fodder, and I like my stable as clean as the kitchen. The tiled walls have to be cleaned daily and the muck wheeled away from the standings."

Sep listened and just replied, "I'll do my best, Sir."

Lewes, who lived in the bothy at the stables, called Sep aside and asked him into his room, a utility room where the groom ate and slept close to the loose boxes where the mares foaled.

The place was so tidy that Sep thought Lewes had expected important visitors. The cooking grate shone with black lead. Two iron saucepans stood on the hobs. An iron kettle swung from pot hooks above the glowing coal. On the mantelpiece above, Lewes kept his tea caddy and tobacco jar. A corner cupboard of stained deal held his provisions.

On the white-washed walls hanging from nails were pictures of horses, huntsmen, hounds. Over his camp bed was a faded photograph of a young soldier smart with waxed moustache, puttied and spurred. At the bottom of the picture were the words 'Trooper Lewes 1840'.

The evening came on with failing light.

"Sit down, Sep, I've finished work for to-day," the groom said, as he offered a chair close to the fire. Sep sat down and Lewes drew up a small scrubbed deal table and placed it between them. "A drop of beer and a hand of cards, boy? Or do you play cards?" Lewes asked the strapper.

"Oh yes, Mr Lewes, I play. You have got a comfortable lodging in here," he said, looking at the shining bridle bits and some horse brasses near the sink where the brass water tap shone.

Lewes lit the oil lamp and told Sep that the brood mares were out in the fields suckling their foals and the loose boxes were empty, but that in May and June sometimes he was up all night with a foaling mare.

"Now, my boy," he said, "our job this Autumn is to see that the Major and his friends have some good mounts for the hunting season. Then we will be training one or two Point-to-Pointers for the Spring and a couple of useful steeplechasers for the Major's nephew to ride in the Amateur Riders' races.''

"The Major's not married I take it.''

"No, but he's had some ladies of class staying at the Grange at times. You see, Sep, his life's been the Army same as me, and neither of us has been married. I'll say this though, the ladies at the Grange have always been good to me. I was ill a while back and they looked after me, called me Mr Lewes.''

"What does the Major call you as a rule, Mr Lewes?'' Sep was inquisitive to know.

"Lewes, of course. I'm still an old trooper, but that's no disrespect, mind. You never think of being called anything different in the Army.''

With this the groom laughed, looked at Sep's round boyish face and said, "You will be 'Sands', young strapper, but I'll call you Sep if that will make you feel more at home. Where are you going to live?''

"At the Cider Mill with Mr and Mrs Badger, not far away.''

Sep explained that he was staying there instead of with Widow Prew, and that Mrs Badger was like a mother to him.

"I'm not looking after you very well,'' Lewes said, "I did say we would have some beer.'' So the old trooper got up from the table and filled two pint pots of a foaming brew.

"There, lad,'' he said, "have a drop of that and I'll deal out the cards.'' So they played and drank, laughed and talked the evening away.

Sep needed someone like Lewes to keep him straight. Lewes was a kind man, but stood no nonsense. His loyalty to the Major was just the same as when he served under him in the Cavalry. He didn't click his heels to attention, and salute in the stable yard, but the quality of a disciplined trooper remained.

When Sep Sands settled in at the Cider Mill, Mr Badger told him straight how fortunate he was to find employment with the Major in the same village where he had been such a poacher.

So the strapper learnt the art of schooling horses under Lewes. He liked the smell of leather, the brilliant brass and silver on the harness. Early mornings he went with Lewes and a string of horses up on Netherstone Hill. Lewes first of all mounted Sep on an old Point-to-Pointer which he took over the jumps on Netherstone Knap; jumps that were made of hurdles laced with gorse.

Then the younger horses like Mettle were tried at the jumps.

It was an experience Sep would never forget, to ride such well-bred, well-looked-after animals, just as the larks rose and the peewits called and when the grass was drenched with dew.

"Ah," he thought as the rabbits scurried to their holes, "poaching was never worth it, this is the life." He looked down at the shining stirrups, his boots and leggings blacked, the cream coloured leather inside the knees of his Bedford cord breeches. His knees gripped leather against the leather saddle.

Lewes knew the feeling—it had happened to him forty years ago.

"Ah, strapper, the Major likes us to look smart when we are out with his horses and I must say just ride as I have shown you, long stirrups, straight back cavalry style, that's how he likes it, none of this short stirrup riding crouching over the horse's mane like a Tom Tit on a leg of mutton."

Sep understood, but did think of pictures he had seen in the racing papers, where jockeys rode in what Lewes called the new fashion.

Back in the stable Lewes and Sep changed into working clothes and combed and brushed the frothy sweat off the horses' backs, shoulders and cruppers.

Then off to breakfast when the corn and chaff had been put in the mangers. When they were back after their meal, the Major arrived and looked around.

"How's Mettle shaping? Does he jump well? Is he a natural?" Lewes smiled, and looked at Sep but quickly answered the Major, the words coming as if rehearsed over breakfast.

"Mettle's a good jumper, and our young strapper cleared the gorse this morning with feet to spare, I reckon you have a good gelding there, Sir, and how he shaped this morning, Mettle's name will be in the paper when your nephew rides him in the Amateur Riders chase."

"By gad, Sands, that will be a feather in your hat. Still, that horse is temperamental so just humour him, Sands, that's all."

As the Major left the stable Lewes put the rugs on two hunters and he and Sep saddled one of them.

"Now, young fella, these two will be hunting in a day or two, and they need no schooling, just exercise, you can ride one and have the leading rein on the other, and keep to the roads. The hard roads will do their hooves good. Take them almost to Oatfield, then turn back along Umberlands Lane past the old Pike house, and home."

Sep looked pleased at the prospect and asked Lewes if he should canter or trot.

"Just trot," Lewes replied.

As Sep left the yard dressed again in his best riding outfit, he glanced at the navy blue rugs on the horses' backs and saw in gold embroidery above the hind quarters the letters, big letters A.F. "Adrian Forbrooke of course," he thought.

It was restful jogging along the country roads looking at the crops over the hedges, and knowing that his two horses were reliable.

He had gone about a mile when he noticed a pretty girl coming towards him carrying a small basket. "Good morning," she said. "I must say you do look smart and how sleek the horses are! You are Sep, aren't you? Is your leg all right now, or shouldn't I ask?"

Sep who had poached, gambled, drank and had his rough and tumble with the village girls, blushed at Gwen. Something he could not explain made him almost speechless, then he stammered, "Yes, I am Sep, and my leg is better, thank you. It was nice of you to inquire. Are you going to the shop?"

Gwen, seeing the effect she had had on Sep, hurried away, but said as she went, "I'm glad you are back in Netherstone."

Sep went on his journey, thinking all the time that he would be meeting so many village people as he exercised the horses. "It's funny," he thought, "how people will speak when you are riding."

Of course Sep was right, because it does give a sort of dignity to anyone to be on a good mount, especially a young man like Sep.

"How bist, young fella? I see thee hast got a horse to ride, daresay you fancied yerself as the Squire." It was Garnet Bullin looking over the hedge where his sheep were penned. He was plastering red raddle on the breast part of a ram before he turned it loose with his ewes.

"All right, Garnet, I'm under groom for the Major," Sep answered.

Garnet loosed the ram and walked to the field gate and teasing said, "It might be an idea to plaster some raddle on your wescut. I see ya a feow minutes agu a hanging yer hat up to young Gwen. Still, thee bist out a the running. Wilf's sweet on her and she doan't seem to mind his courting."

6

The New Reaper

TOM SAMSON FOR YEARS HAD HIS CORN CUT BY BAG-ging hooks and wooden hooks or pitchthanks. By hook and by crook, Garnet had called it as he and Nailus circled the wheat fields in August, leaving rows of sheaves for the village women to tie with straw bands.

This summer Tom had bought a reaper at the Agricultural Show. Its agitating blade left a short stubble, and the untied sheaves were laid in rows around the field.

Tom had also bought two young horses at the March Fair. Nailus had planted the corn with them; these five-year-olds were handy, but had never drawn a reaper. He was dubious about putting these two horses on a machine, which he said chattered like a lot of blasted hens about to lay, and that the sails which laid the cut corn behind the knife reminded him of 'One a these yer windmills as I a sin pictures of from Holland'.

"They tells me," he said, "that nothing good comes from there Dutch courage, for hinstance. It's alus was done be hand in fayther's time and it allus got done be Michaelmas. Still, young Tom a bought this yer himplement, but I'm dammed if I be gwain to get on the seat."

Joe Badger listened intently to Nailus in the bar, and said, "I'll ride the reaper if Master Samson wants a hand."

The day before the reaping started, Nailus and his brother cut a road around the wheat field. This they did using the bagging hooks. They tied the sheaves and stood them against the hedge. 'Opening up' they called it, leaving enough cleared stubble for two horses to walk abreast without treading on the standing corn.

"What dos't think a this new menagerie, you?" Garnet said as he looked round the reaper in the rickyard.

Nailus took his pipe from his lips and spat. Then pointing with his reaping hook to the sails, he looked at Garnet and said, "I be very much afraid as that whirlygig ull knock a smartish bit of grain from the ripe ears of wheat."

Next morning Joe Badger was helped by Nailus to hitch the horses to the machine, as soon as the morning dew had dried on the head-land. Tom Samson's two young horses, Turpin and Sharper, stepped forward together beside the standing grain. The knife rattled its way through the straw shearing everything before it, and just leaving a six-inch high stubble.

Tom Samson's new 'side delivery reaper' mowed the corn leaving it in a tidy swath for the tyers to tie into sheaves. The machine was magic to the old men of Netherstone, who came down to the field to see Tom Samson's reaper.

Around the standing corn men and women stood at intervals to tie the sheaves with straw bands. Nailus and Garnet worked together, suspicious of the implement which had taken from them the task of hand reaping.

Jane and Kate tied their sheaves with the same straw knot as they had used for years behind the reaping hooks of Garnet and Nailus.

Widow Prew was there and Mary Badger, who came for part of the day. There was a feeling that Mary came to see that no harm befell Joe as he sat like captain of a ship on his seat beside the sails.

Squire Mathison released Wilf from his work with the game in the woods to tie sheaves with Gwen. Annette the lady of the Manor, agreed to manage for one day without her personal maid, a small farmer's daughter from Brecon.

"All go, yunt it?" Nailus said to his brother as Joe made another circuit of the cornfield. Garnet threw his waistcoat on the hedge and bent down once more among the mown wheat. His back showed fawncords up to his braces which crossed his shoulders like the harness of a horse, leather braces they were, worn smooth over his striped shirt.

"Oi, buoy," he said, "it ull never be the same agun now this yalla and red article a started cutting the corn."

Nailus watched his two young horses pull and sweat and snort. Winking at his brother he remarked, "Now there's a pair of decent shires fit to go in any horse show."

Garnet laughed as he knotted yet another sheaf, and the sweat dropped from his nose.

"Yes," he said. "You was must afraid to ride on the seat behind um though I recon. Joe Badger has got the laugh over you to-day, he riding round like a toff a gwain to town and thee at this back-breaking job tying sheaves."

The cider from the cool hedgerow was poured from the jar into the horn tots and thirsts were laxed and tales exchanged.

"Yonder, look!" shouted Nailus. "Young Wilf a skylarking with Gwen, it is good to be young, no ties like we put around the sheaves."

Wilf sat under an oak tree sipping tea from the blue top of an enamel tea can (Gwen had brought the tea from the Manor). Then as she drank from the same cup which formed the lid of the can, Wilf plaited straw into her hair and was shoved away in a playful manner.

"Look ya," Garnet called to his brother, "Wilf a drinking cat lap with the Welsh wench," and raising his voice called towards the oak tree:

"Come on now, let's get on with the work, plenty a time for that kind of thing after dark."

Mary Badger spoke quietly to Widow Prew as they bound the sheaves, telling her how much Gwen reminded her of Ruth in the Bible. "Not that we are leasing or gleaning as it says in the Book, but surely Wilf and Annette's maid do make a handsome pair."

"Ah," Widow Prew replied, "they do and I wish with all my heart they marry. My man died, but I'll never forget him.

It's a lonely life sitting at the table by yourself and having no one to share the fireside with, but the cat on the rag rug.''

"Sep will make someone a good husband when treated right, but he's not just the one for Gwen. She has told him so already, you know."

As the men and women laboured in the midday sun the sound of the hunting horn came from the coppice by Benedict's Pool. Nailus straightened his back and told his neighbours in his own particular way that 'The Huntsmans' was calling the hounds from the spinney to go home from cub hunting.

"They be late to-day," Garnet added. "The meet was at about seven this morning."

The Major from the Grange led the field down Netherstone Hill, the pack followed the huntsman, and the few followers who indulged in cub hunting followed the Major who was riding on Mettle, and Sep on a younger horse. Squire Mathison, Rev Cuthbert, a few boys on shaggy ponies, and a fine young lady of about twenty-three riding a bay mare three-quarters thorough-bred.

She wore a black bowler over her curls, smiled and waved her riding crop at the reapers.

"Who might that be?" Garnet asked.

Aaron Hicks was opening the gate for the horses and Aaron was always a bit careful in stating who rode over his Master's land. He knew that Garnet would talk with a loosened tongue in the Cider Mill about anything he had heard during the day, when he sat in Badgers' kitchen at night.

So "Just a lady from the next village," Aaron said. "Nice horse, don't you think?"

Garnet watched the Major and Sep ride close to the lady, then he muttered to Nailus in a sort of fatalistic way about some chaps having all the luck.

The weather held fine as Tom Samson brought Captain and Colonel into the field at dinner time. He and Joe unhitched Turpin and Sharper wiping the foaming sweat from under their collars with a cloth, and put his two old horses on the reaper.

It's true the knife didn't chatter as fast as when Joe rode the machine but Tom went steadily around the field of wheat, the standing corn making an even smaller island in the sea of golden stubble around.

Men and women of Netherstone who had tied the sheaves now sat in groups in the shade, eating their bait or midday meal.

Nailus looked eagerly towards the clothed pudding basins as Kate undid the string.

"A nice bit of brawn for you," she said, and the harvester and his elder brother ate like lords under the hawthorn hedge.

Joe brought back the young horses in the afternoon and finished cutting the field by teatime. He and Tom Samson helped to tie the remainder of the sheaves, and as the moon rose over Netherstone Hill the two brothers, 'the Bullins', walked wearily to the cool of Joe Badger's kitchen at the Cider Mill.

"Who was that lady thing on that bay mare cub hunting to-day, riding alongside young Sep?" Mary Badger was half expecting this question from Garnet, and she was ready with a guarded answer. She knew that as long as Joe and herself lived at the Cider Mill and made a living at what was known as the village 'Public' how careful her answers had to be.

"The lady," Mary told Garnet, "is a young widow from a few miles away. She lost her husband when he contracted typhoid fever in Africa. He was out there with a gold mining company."

"Rich, I'll warrant?" Garnet gasped over his pint pot.

Mary turned in the bar as she replied curtly, "That's all I know, that she is a widow, and if Rosemary Ransome likes Major Forbrooke's company that's not our business."

7

Autumn at the Manor

AARON AND WILF HAD GOT THE REARED PHEASANTS
settled in the woods on Netherstone Hill. They still fed them,
although the stubbles on Samson's farm provided a good picking
after harvest for both pheasants and partridge.

Annette's parents came down on the London train, and stayed
with her and the Squire, her mother bringing her maid from her
London house, and her father spent his time hunting and shooting
from the Manor.

Garnet and Nailus cropped Tom Samson's hedges, always
leaving cover at intervals for guns to stand behind waiting the
driven partridges. The guns of course being the invited guests of
the Squire; his tenant Tom was one of them. These hides or
butts were trimmed to about five feet high, whereas the rest of
the hedge was about three feet. Stations at intervals like this
broke the even pattern of hedges but were essential to hide the
shooting men from the partridges.

The local doctor came to these shoots, and was most accurate
with his gun. Annette herself was a useful shot with her twenty-
bore double-barrelled, hammer gun.

Nailus, Garnet, Aaron, Wilf and other men and boys from the
village were always pleased when a covey of birds flew towards
her. They knew that she would show her skill to the gentlemen,
and get her share of the day's bag.

When the Saturdays in October echoed with shots fired at the
pheasants as they flew from cover to cover, Aaron and Wilf were
busy late in the evening picking up the game. Then again on
Sundays. The retriever dogs worked through the woods with the

keepers, picking up the birds they had missed and those which had unfortunately been winged.

All through the week Nailus ploughed the stubbles with his young horses Turpin and Sharper. They stepped along at a quicker pace than the old ones and by three o'clock the carter was glad to sit on the stable bench and rest his tired legs while the horses ate the bait (a mixture of chaff and corn) from the manger and pulled the sweet clover from the hay rack.

Tom Samson would come in and smile, knowing that Nailus had asked for young horses but felt now that he was getting to be an old ploughman.

"Young Wilf don't get out along with Gwen lately, Gaffer," Nailus said. "Don't fancy her any more?"

Tom sat by his ploughman on the bench, saying "Look here, you and me have had our day with the girls. I daresay Wilf and Gwen will be together again. Wilf's been busy, you know, with the shoots and no doubt Gwen has plenty to do at the Manor."

"Oi," Nailus chuckled.

He was right, of course, Wilf, who lived at Samson's farm, had not been seeing Gwen. Tom and Sarah were sorry about this; they knew how Wilf felt, a newcomer to Netherstone, how he thought that the farmer's daughter from Brecon was being schooled by Annette so that one day she would be Bob Cuthbert the Vicar's wife.

Wilf was jealous of the Vicar, but knew that Sep Sands was out of the running. Gwen had told Sep and Sep understood.

The Harvest Festival was over at the church. The usual competition between Garnet and Joe Badger as to who could grow the biggest marrow had been decided. Joe won this year by half a pound weight, but the two marrows had lain as close friends. "And they bears no malice whose marrow's the biggest, now unt that Christian?" said Nailus to the Vicar.

"Of course, Nailus," he replied. "That's what it's all about. We gather together here year by year in early October to thank God for the harvest. Your sickle is by the font, I see."

"Oi," Nailus said. "We hadn't got room for that implement as cut the main corn this year, but you must excuse an old man's logic when I tells ya that Gwen's solo was like listening to angels so to speak."

Rev Cuthbert changed the subject straight away, having seen quite a lot of Gwen at choir practice with Annette accompanying her on the organ.

"Yes, Nailus, a great institution Rev Hawker started in Cornwall when he held the first Harvest Festival."

"Oi spose so," Nailus nodded, "but when be we gwain to have the feed?"

"Oh you mean the Supper? The Squire and Mr Samson have it in hand. Tom and Mary Badger are catering, you will get your feed, Nailus."

The following week the Squire sent Aaron, Wilf and his estate workers down to Tom Samson's big barn where Nailus, Garnet, Joe and a few lads were cleaning it ready for the harvest supper. That night the loaded plates of beef, ham and pickles lay in rows on the trestle tables. The big apple pies baked by Annette and Gwen were brought from the Manor. Joe and Mary tapped a barrel of best beer, and rows of candles lit the tables, while horn lanterns hung from the huge cross timbers in the cobwebbed arch of the roof.

The Squire was in the chair accompanied by Major Forbrooke, and the ladies included the young widow of the next village. Annette sat at a piano.

Rev Cuthbert said grace, a longer one than usual. He gave thanks for Netherstone country, and reminded his flock it had not always been such a harvest; there had been lean years for master and man.

When the feasting and drinking had ended the Squire gave a toast to the Queen; Mrs Ransome, the young widow, thanked the Squire on behalf of the visitors.

Jane Bullin, who with Kate had helped to wait at the tables, was worried about Garnet. He insisted on telling the young wife of the Squire of his love affairs, and how he romped with the girls on Netherstone Hill when he was but a lad.

"I'm sorry, mam, but 'tis the liquor. I do hope he says nothing to offend you," Jane said.

"Don't worry, Jane, Garnet's amusing me, but such goings on, I am surprised."

The usual songs were sung. Garnet staggered to the piano and bawled "Some calls I bacon face," then put his arm around Annette and kissed her saying, "Yers to the Squire's young wife, 'God Bless Her'."

The evening passed. The plates were cleared and all except Garnet made their way home.

"I be mortal ashamed a my man," Kate said to Annette as Garnet lay on a truss of hay in the corner of the barn, mouth wide open, fast asleep, his empty mug fallen to the barn floor.

Annette laughed and helped Kate to get him to his feet, and they both held his arms and walked him to the cottage while he sang 'The Farmer's Boy'.

Wilf's eyes had been on Gwen's as she helped with the supper. His heart was set on her, but the last thing he wanted was to appear to be forcing himself on her, to be cheap and pushing. "Oh dear," he thought, as she and the Vicar had chatted so freely. "Gwen's probably looking for a husband with more education than a mere under keeper."

Wilf talked to Aaron, standing lantern in hand between the great double doors of the barn. A doorway wide enough and tall enough for the biggest farm waggon to enter.

"Bit sweet on Gwen, aren't you, Wilf?" Aaron said.

Wilf nodded.

"No time like the present. It's courage you need, my boy, and here you are after a supper such as we have had and plenty to drink. A faint heart never won a fair lady," he told his assistant keeper. Then said, "Good night, see you in the morning."

Wilf waited until Gwen came through the doorway. She had slipped her best coat over the wine coloured velvet dress with the lace collar, which had given her figure such elegance at supper.

"Gwen," he said, "are you in a hurry?"

"Not particular, Wilf. Have you enjoyed everything to-night?"

"Well, yes I have, but I just wondered whether we could walk together up the footpath to Benedict's Pool."

Gwen thought a little while, and kept him waiting for an answer. An answer which she had decided immediately.

Wilf cleared his throat, and muttered, "I suppose it's a bit late?"

"No," came the reply. "But I must get Mrs Mathison's permission."

At that moment Annette crossed the cobbled yard by the granary steps and past the barn towards the Manor.

"Can I stay out late tonight, please?" Gwen asked her.

Annette stopped as she replied, "I can guess Wilf has asked you out on Netherstone Hill. Of course you can stay out. Stay out like I did in France, until the small hours of the morning. I'd rather you be with Wilf than anyone. Good night each. Here's the key, Gwen, enjoy yourself."

Wilf and Gwen first of all went to the Manor, where Gwen put on stronger shoes than the ones she had worn at the supper matching her dress, shiny shoes with silvery buckles.

The couple left. Wilf's lantern was douted in the dairy, and they walked under a crescent moon up the worn footpath to Netherstone Hill, and the Pool.

The moon and stars gave just enough light between the stone walls on the hill.

Wilf boldly put his arm around the waist of the Welsh girl.

"What are you thinking?" she said.

"Oh, lots of things are going through my mind. I'm just happy. Happy to be with you just for one night, and can we come up here often?"

Gwen laughed. "Of course, why not? There's nothing I'd like better than to spend my evenings with you."

As Wilf threw both his strong arms around her their lips met in the half light of the moon. He pressed his mouth gently against hers.

He felt as he had never felt before. Strong legs which had daily worked on Netherstone Hill trembled, as her arms clung to his waist. All conversation stopped for what seemed minutes until Wilf whispered, "Darling, will you be mine, just mine?"

Gwen kissed him firmly, and as their lips parted she said, "Always, Wilf, if you love me."

The couple of lovers had not got far up the hill, but Wilf had promised to walk to Benedict's Pool, and on they went up the footpath saying very little, but now Gwen also had an arm around Wilf. Every hundred yards or so they stopped, kissed and then went on. Over the stone hill stile they heard the mallard quacking on the Pool. The hill was theirs for that night, all the folk at Netherstone had gone to their beds.

Near Benedict's Pool an outcrop of limestone formed a shelf in the hill, a natural seat. I suppose most of the natives of Netherstone had sat there, boys and girls together, except of course when the moon was full, and the ducks left; then it was said to be eerie.

Wilf placed his overcoat on the stone seat, Gwen sat beside him.

Wilf was bolder now away from the village, away from inquisitive Nailus and Garnet. He had even been uneasy in the Vicar's company, knowing that Rev Cuthbert probably thought as much of Gwen as he did. Then Wilf thought again, reassuring himself that this could never be possible. No, Gwen to him was everything, there could never be anyone in the world like her.

As they sat on the coat in each other's arms, Wilf's heart throbbed as fast as his pocket watch. Gwen's breast was soft against his waistcoat, it heaved as she sighed. They clung together tighter still until Gwen fell limply towards him, laying her head on his shoulder so that Wilf had nearly the weight of her whole body on his lap.

"Oh Wilf," she said. "Let it always be like this between you and me, I do love you so."

"Gwen, my angel," Wilf said. "Do you also trust me, because never will there be anyone but you in my life."

"Of course," Gwen replied as her face turned from his shoulder and she kissed his neck. Wilf thought how wonderful it all was and wondered whether other young men like himself had had the same experience.

His hands slid to the mother-of-pearl buttons on her dress and softly his fingers held her breast. Gwen sighed and whispered:

"That's lovely! Wilf, what made you do that?"

"Don't know," Wilf whispered, "I just want to be so close to you."

"I can trust you, Wilf, can't I? Because you can, well, hold my other breast."

Wilf undid the front of her dress until he felt a soft silky part of her body which was like a rounded cushion. His fingers touched the nipple.

Gwen murmured, "Promise you won't go farther."

"God's honour, Gwen, I'd do nothing to you that was against your wish."

And so they lay on the limestone seat by the pool with just the occasional quack of the wild ducks and the chatter of moorhens, the plop of the fish as they surfaced.

"Do you believe in heaven?" Gwen asked.

"Yes, Gwen, I do, and angels. When I heard you sing at the Harvest Festival, I heard angels, and you are an angel, Gwen. I'll sleep at night now I know you love me, because for weeks I've been waking and wondering about you, Gwen."

Gwen closed her eyes as she lay there and then said, "Wilf, there will be another evening up here soon. We really ought to go you know."

Wilf buttoned up her dress, stroked her ruffled hair, brushed her coat and together they took the path to Netherstone.

As Gwen turned the key in the back door of the Manor, she

thought of nothing but that Wilf and she were in love. Wilf went to his bed at Samson's farm, a happy, contented man. He could already imagine Gwen the other side of a fireplace in their own home.

8

Some Puzzles of Nature

THE PEOPLE OF NETHERSTONE HAD ALWAYS BEEN ready to accept natural disasters. When Tom Samson's father had liver fluke among his sheep and lost a lot of ewes, this was the result of a wet season. But the old folk still talked of the great mortality of 1729, and the facts handed down from father to son were considered sinister. Forty-five people died between Christmas and May, all suddenly from swellings of the throat. This was different, no wonder people were superstitious.

A parson of long ago preached against the village folk who broke the Sabbath Day, and when the service was over two young Netherstone men played with cudgels in the church-yard. Almost immediately one had his eye struck out.

"Yer's evidence without doubt that One above ull have His vengeance," Garnet told Nailus. "You can't trifle along with Him, mind tha."

"Well, thee bist a cheerful chap," said Nailus, who liked to question his brother on such points. "That could have happened on any day."

This summer had been so hot and dry that the cattle pulled the herbs from the hedges when all the brown grass had been eaten. The grazing fields were bare and the land cracked. Men were lopping the boughs from withy trees to let the cows eat the leaves.

Netherstone Hill looked like a barren desert, parched by the summer sun. The light crop of hay was slippery as Tom Samson's pitchers forked their shuppicks full of over dry herbage on the waggons. The weather was so hot that as the grass fell behind the blade the new mown hay could have been carried the same day.

"It is to be hoped we has a mild winter, Gaffer," Nailus told Mr Samson. "The ricks be devilish small this season."

Tom Samson told Garnet to thatch every rick as soon as it was settled down because he wanted to avoid any wastage from the Autumn rain, if the rain came.

The cattle, sheep and horses seemed to thrive on the meagre grass of the fields. Netherstone Hill was fortunate in having an ample supply of water gushing from the springs. There by the stream, and in the stream where the lime in the water turned the fallen elder sticks into a soft stone, the watercress grew.

In his poaching days Sep had taken this palatable green salad to the Cider Mill and sold it to the questionable dealers in game, mushrooms and anything they could get.

Every afternoon in that short period between haymaking and harvest Garnet's face shone like the blazing sun and the sweat ran in streams from his nose as he pegged the thatch on the hayricks. His flannel shirt was soaked with sweat, and if the rick was away from the yard, in some field corner perhaps, he would hang the sodden flannel on the hawthorn hedge like gipsy's washing, and the sun dried it while he worked with a waistcoat on to cover his bare back.

The heat became still more intense, the bree flies worried the cattle from midday until the evening cool. Poor beasts could be seen in Netherstone meadows circling a trodden path near the hedges, their tails erect trying in vain to escape from the torment of the worrying flies.

At last, with foaming mouths and lolling tongues, they bored their way between the rough bushes in the corner of the field, and stood switching their tails as close to each other as in a market pen.

For several nights as Netherstone folk lay uncovered in bed in rooms where the tiles had been heated by the sun, their little dolls' house windows hooked open wide to let in the slightest breeze, lightning flickered over the distant hills, but it was miles away and not a rumble of thunder was heard.

Garnet and Jane tossed on their flock mattress. As sleep came at last, it was for just a short interlude when their tired bodies and minds were lost to the world. Garnet lit a candle, looked at his watch and the great night moths known as 'Bobhowluds' came for the lighted candle and singed their wings. As Garnet turned in bed he muttered to Jane: ˑ

"If the rain don't soon come everything ull be parched up, no taters for the winter."

"You still believe in the Almighty's promise, Garnet, about seedtime and harvest."

Garnet sighed. "S'pose so," he said. "Although my shepherding prevents me from going to church regular."

Getting up once more Garnet climbed Netherstone Hill very early in the morning, the brown grass wet with dew damping his boots.

He thought as he looked at the straight lines of red on the almost cloudless sky line that the great ball of fire which he had heard Bob Cuthbert call Phoebus would soon be shining from the East.

Garnet's sheep nibbled comfortably at the dewy grass. Their damp fleeces would soon be hot and greasy again. What seemed to be an eternal Summer had come to Netherstone.

Rev Bob Cuthbert no longer spent his evenings from afternoon tea until bedtime in his sunny dining-room, but retreated to the coolness of Hannah's kitchen. Hannah, the Vicar's aunt, was housekeeper at Netherstone Vicarage.

Here the stone slabbed floor and thick walls with a lattice window facing north made life more pleasant, so Bob and Hannah had tea there and dined on the scrubbed table by the up-turned buckets and the butter churn.

Tom Samson knew that he would be short of fodder for the Winter; every bent of hay would be wanted. There was a little meadow by the brook which he didn't often mow, but kept for Autumn grazing for the horses.

"Mow the Stonebridge Meadow," he told Nailus one morning in the stable.

"What about my horses, Gaffer, at Michaelmas?" Nailus said, raising his eyebrows. "We allus depends on that bit of grass keep."

Tom Samson understood, but explained to his carter that when the rain came, the grass would grow with the land so hot.

Nailus mowed the meadow in the morning and he and Garnet loaded the hay on two waggons the same evening. That is to say, they pitched the hay to Tom Samson who loaded from the pitchforks.

"Yonder, Gaffer!" Garnet shouted, making the three men look towards the brook. A whirlwind had lifted a forkful of hay which went up like a balloon out of sight.

"Tempest," Garnet said. "We be just in time—the weather's about to break."

The hay was taken by Nailus and his horses to the rick-yard and unloaded into the empty bay of the barn next to the stable.

As the men went home that night a breeze got up; such a welcome change to the stifling evenings of the last eight weeks. The lightning sheeted over the hills accompanied by a faint rumble of thunder.

It was one o'clock when the storm drew near from Benedict's Pool. The lightning licked the larches like tongues of fire, the crackle and rumble of thunder was continuous.

No one stayed in bed in the village that night; something eerie about the place made it impossible for the folk to stay there.

Lewes and Sep dressed and went to the stable, staying with the mares and foals, carrying extra feed for them to settle them, for every time a crash of thunder sounded like cannon the horses pottered in their loose boxes, and Lewes saw the whites of their eyes by lantern light.

Rev Cuthbert and Hannah sat together on the drawing-room sofa, the window curtains open, and watched the electric display.

Hannah was afraid of the crash of thunder and when the lightning shot its flaming arrows seemingly into the paddock she shielded her eyes. Robert consoled her, assuring her that no harm would come to them.

"You see," he said, "when the lightning conductor, that copper rod higher than the church tower, was installed, a previous Vicar had one put on the tall chimney of the Vicarage."

No rain came and how Tom Samson longed for a steady down-pour everyone knew. He stood in the rickyard with Sarah and Wilf and marvelled at the way the whole of the landscape was lit up by every flash of lightning. They saw the top of Nether-stone Hill, the trees around the Pool.

Aaron at his cottage in the wood sat and smoked his pipe in the kitchen. The pheasants were calling from the trees as if dawn had come three hours too soon.

As Major Forbrooke rode his horse furiously through the night to keep Rosemary Ransome company, his thoughts were two-fold. In the first instance he was genuinely fond of her, but also he knew how pleased she would be of his kind thought of her safety.

The Squire, Annette and Gwen sat around a table playing cards under the oil lamp. Widow Prew ran to the Cider Mill after the thunder had made the window-panes tartle so in the cottage.

Never in the remembrance of man had such thunder and lightning shattered the peaceful night at Netherstone.

Garnet and Jane went next door to Nailus and Kate's cottage.

Garnet was uneasy about his sheep on Netherstone Hill. The rain dropped in spots as big as halfpennies on the cobbled path. Slowly at first it came, starting and stopping, but over Benedict's

Pool the sky was a black backcloth to the forked spears of golden fire from the clouds.

"My ship, my yows and lambs be in the walled field where the beech trees be," he said.

"Well, what can you do?" Jane asked.

Garnet looked down at the flagstone floor of the kitchen. "Take Rosie my dog, and drive um away from the trees, and pen um in the barn, then I can bide with them in the barn until this lot's over. They huddle together under the beeches, I'm sure, and like enough get struck down with lightning. Where's my heavy cloak, missus, I be gwain up to anant the Benedict's Pool. Come on, Rosie."

"I be mortal worried," Jane said, "of you going out in this lot."

Garnet took his crook, and well wrapped up against the rain walked up the path to the top of Netherstone Hill.

When he left the lightning grew more and more intense, while in the storm overhead the forks from cloud to earth turned purple instead of red. The whole skyscape was angry, the thunder cannoned louder shaking the barns and houses. The rain turned to a cloudburst which brought streams of water down the hill through the Vicarage garden and flooded the church. The houses and cottages were flooded in varying degrees. Only Aaron's place in the wood lay dry, as the torrents roared down the willow-lined gully to the village.

"Two o'clock I makes it," Nailus told his wife and sister-in-law. "Garnet ull be in the big barn along with his sheep now."

Jane was anxious and kept saying, "I wish my man was here, he should never gone out tonight."

The thunder moved to the distant hills before dawn and rumbled like waggon wheels down a lane. The lightning was now just sheets of yellow in the distance.

When the first light of day came from the angry sky the scene in Netherstone was worse than anyone expected. The hard, parched land, unable to absorb such a quantity of water, was flooded. Partridges' young ones were drowned in the furrows, rabbits in their burrows. The church was ankle deep in mud and water. Great elm trees lay like soldiers after a battle across the lanes. But what of Garnet? He hadn't come home.

Tom Samson called in the stable, "Nailus, where's Garnet? Jane says he's not back off the hill."

"No, Gaffer, he yunt, and Jane's worried amus' to death about him; he should be back for his breakfast."

Tom Samson was anxious too, and told Nailus to leave his horses and come up the hill and look for his brother.

Together they walked the footpath and were puzzled where to look first for Garnet.

"Like enough he's asleep in the shepherd's hut near the Pool, Master Samson. He has bin known to have a nap in there on the corn sacks. Mind ya," Nailus went on, "he'd be tired by the time he'd penned the sheep in the barn."

"Oh, that's what he was going to do, was it? But what a dreadful night," Tom added, "and I never seen the streams run like they do to-day."

At Benedict's Pool the water gushed brown from the hill and frothed as it swilled the limestone track.

"He unt in there," Nailus said as he undid the asp and staple of the hut.

"We better go to the barn then." Tom was very worried now. "And see what's happened."

Across two walled fields the old barn stood empty. The ewes and lambs grazed the washed grass while every so often a ewe would shake herself like a wet dog sending spray off her fleece.

"Looks like a bough has blowed off one of the beech trees," Nailus broke the silence. A silence between master and man which had lasted longer than usual after not finding Garnet in the barn.

"Ah, Nailus, it's a sorry sight on the hill and vale this morning. See the corn flattened before it's ripe down by the railway line, and the telegraph wires down, but that's nothing compared with what's happened to your brother my shepherd.''

Under the beech trees past the barn was a circular wall built in stone. The wall was low and served no useful purpose except to form a boundary to a hollow in the hill.

The beeches had been planted in a ring around the wall; this enclosure could have been an old dew pond, no one ever knew. Some of Tom Samson's ewes and lambs had sheltered on this spot from the tempest and cloudburst of the early morning.

The fallen branch had landed clear of the circle, but under the tree lay about six ewes and their lambs dead, stiff and sodden.

Their carcases had already started to blow up to twice their size as they had filled with gases.

Tom looked at Nailus, full of pity, full of anguish, as he saw Garnet lying stretched out on the turf still holding his crook, and Rosie his dog by the side of him, both dead.

A seam of peeled bark, scorched, was torn from the tree, the wood underneath was brown and burnt.

A pattern of beech leaves had tattooed the shepherd's face as he lay there struck by the lightning.

Nailus bent over his brother and cried like a child. ''All these years together he and me, but he has died in harness,'' he sobbed.

Tom didn't know what to say, but knew that Nailus would understand.

He leant down and felt Garnet's cold brow, picked up his lifeless hand, stood over the shepherd with clasped hands and said, ''Farewell, my friend, you have been a good shepherd, you put your flock first. . . . Shall we go, Nailus? I'll see the Squire and arrange for Wilf and Aaron to bring him down in the game cart.''

Nailus turned away and fetched a sack from the barn.

''I'll cover his face up, Gaffer, you know how the carrion birds ull go for the eyes of a corpse.''

At Samson's cottage Jane and Kate were wringing their hands in despair when Tom Samson went with the news.

"Is he dead, Mr Samson?" Jane met Garnet's employer at the gate.

"I'm afraid so, Jane. Struck by lightning along with his dog and some of the sheep. Wilf and Aaron are bringing him down."

Kate was a great comfort to Jane and talked quietly of how Garnet had died at his work, a work he loved.

Nailus came in and said how sorry he was for Jane, then put the kettle on and made a pot of tea.

Netherstone village was struck dumb by the news. Joe Badger passed the church bell. Widow Prew came along as the game cart with Aaron and Wilf brought Garnet to the cottage, and put him in the front room. Jane said as Nailus led her to the back kitchen:

"You'd best to see him when Widow Prew have done the necessary."

Aaron and Wilf carried the now stiff body of Garnet into the parlour where the doctor from Oatfield as a matter of form pronounced him dead.

Then Widow Prew laid him out and the family came in and saw the old labourer of Netherstone at rest at last.

Bob Cuthbert came, Annette brought Jane a bottle of port wine and persuaded her to take a glass or two to keep her spirits from getting too low. Then Jane made a little speech which will never be forgotten in Netherstone. She thanked all her friends and neighbours for the love they had shown to her at this sad occasion.

"Where should I be without you all, Mrs Mathison?" she said to Annette: "We be but poor working folk!" Annette was young and compassionate. The tears streamed down her face and looking at the Vicar she said, "Garnet was a jewel in our parish." Bob Cuthbert nodded as he softly uttered "Amen."

The next two days the sun shone once more and the heat

in the ground made the grass grow; in fact you could almost see it grow green again. As Garnet lay for the last time in his cottage, and the grave was dug, the village wheelwright made a coffin for him.

"Do a decent job," Tom Samson told him. "We will never see his like again."

Jane's two sons came for the funeral. As the bell tolled at two-fifteen for two-thirty p.m. the blinds of the cottages and bigger houses were drawn.

The procession passed through the street to the churchyard, only a short distance. Wilf, Aaron and Lewes pulled the coffin-laden bier smothered with flowers from the gardens.

A touching little incident happened just before the funeral. Nailus spoke to Rev Cuthbert and the wheelwright who was undertaker.

"Now put me right if I be wrong," he said to the Vicar, "but my brother rarely went to church owing to being tied up with his job as shepherd."

"Quite right, I understand," Bob Cuthbert said. "He was as good a living Christian man as any in the parish. What's worrying you, Nailus?"

Nailus looked at the Vicar and said, "It's an old custum you know, to put a wisp or a small handful of wool under a dead shepherd's chin so that when he meets his Maker his Maker ull know he's a shepherd and excuse him from not going to church regular."

"It shall be done, Nailus. A lovely thought, don't you agree, Wheelwright?"

"Yes Sir," the undertaker said. "I've never done it before but that shall be seen to."

And so with Widow Prew at the organ the four carriers of Netherstone wheeled Garnet's coffin into the church.

'The Lord's my Shepherd' they sang together, the Squire, the publican, Gwen and Hannah. Rev Cuthbert read from the Book about the Good Shepherd.

Out in the churchyard Aaron, Wilf, Sep and Lewes lowered the mortal remains of Garnet and pulled back the webbing cords from the coffin. Then as the fine soil of his native village was sprinkled on the box below, Bob Cuthbert read the prayers, and Garnet was buried.

Sarah Samson had prepared refreshments for the mourners and headed by the Vicar they went to the farmhouse.

Here a little group of country folk reflected on the life of Garnet. If the shepherd had been a duke he could not have had a more loving farewell party.

"It has left a gap in Netherstone," the Vicar said, "Garnet was a true son of the soil."

Next day Rev Cuthbert met Nailus at his work in the fields and asked about the scorched shepherd's crook Garnet left behind.

" 'Tis in my washhouse, Vicar," Nailus said. "Why?"

Rev Cuthbert explained that during the service a thought came to him that it would be nice to hang the crook in the vestry and he would have a little inscription placed under it for folk to read in later years how Garnet died at his duty as a Good Shepherd.

After the storm the scene in the village and on the hill was that of devastation. The church was cleared of mud. The fallen trees were sawn and moved from the lanes.

Tom Samson viewed with despair his laid crop of corn.

" 'Tis all down as flat as a pancake," Nailus said to Joe Badger. "It ull mean us cutting it with the hooks again."

Joe thought that the reaper would cut a lot of it, if they had patience and cut towards the laid ears and of course the hot sun would raise it a little off the ground so that the reaper knife could get under it.

In another month things might improve, some said.

Rosemary Ransome rode alone one day on the hill through the bridle gate past the firs and Benedict's Pool. The turf was soft after the rain and slippery in places. She saw the carrion crows and magpies feeding off the carcases of partridges drowned in the furrow, off rabbits swilled from their holes, and was sad. She rode past the beech trees and noticed a man at work burying the dead sheep; it was Aaron Hicks, Squire Mathison's keeper. Riding towards him she inquired about Rosie, Garnet's sheep dog.

"I've buried her, ma'am, in Mr Samson's orchard close against the churchyard wall. She's not far from her old Master. Wilf and I are cutting a wooden cross to put on her grave, wood from the coppices."

"That seems just right," Rosemary said and rode away.

She had not been gone ten minutes and was on the edge of an escarpment above Benedict's Pool when her horse stopped short. Dismounting and noticing the uneasiness of her horse, she saw a deep crack in the hill and that the stile and wall below had moved some yards down the bank. As she looked down the different layers of stone and soil were plain, in even seams.

She rode to the Grange where Major Forbrooke was interested, but also pleased Rosemary was safe. She could so easily have fallen down the crevice.

Sep and Lewes accompanied the other two up the hill again. The Major was interested to know all about the strange happenings. He told Sep to bring a strong waggon rope with him. Arriving at the scene Sep said that he was willing to climb down deep into the hill if Lewes held the rope, and the rope was tied under his arms.

As Sep went lower down among the limestone rock he came to a pot hole full of parched grain. Shouting to the Major telling him of his find he filled the poacher's pocket of his jacket with grain, and as Lewes pulled the rope and helped him to the surface the four of them sorted it over on a horse blanket, finding Roman coins.

"That's it," the Major said. "An old granary, could be Iron Age."

"Roman coins here as well," Rosemary said. "Didn't the Romans hold this hill and the men of the Wicca? How fascinating, Adrian! But how about this great land slip? It's dangerous."

Sep and Lewes looked at the nearby side stone wall and decided that the only way to make the crack in the earth safe would be to fill at least the top part with stone, and they got to work. Rosemary, the Major and Sep carried the stone to Lewes, who bridged the gap in the hill.

"This is only a temporary measure, Sir," he told the Major, "but it will save loss of life, both animal and human."

"Yes," the Major said. "That's the spirit, Lewes. We have lost valuable life here this very week."

They left the site and rode to Benedict's Pool where Rosemary liked to watch the water fowl, and this morning a heron was diving for fish.

Some of the mallard were foraging on the flooded pastures of Netherstone brook, the moorhens and coots among rushes.

"Shall we come often? It's really beautiful here, Adrian," she said.

"It's a lovely spot, ma'am," Lewes replied for the Major, whose thoughts were on Rosemary alone.

9

Nailus's New Neighbour

ALL VILLAGE PEOPLE KNEW THAT TOM SAMSON COULDN'T possibly look after his sizeable flock of sheep for long without a shepherd.

The news of Garnet's death spread around the vale of Netherstone to Oathill and beyond. The local newspaper gave it quite a spread, giving every detail of Garnet's life for his master, the sheep and the land.

Gwen had often helped her father as a girl on the Welsh mountains rounding up the nimble Welsh ewes.

Annette, that girl who always rose to the occasion, a girl mature for her years, suggested to the Squire that Gwen could help Tom with the sheep, and the Squire immediately said that Wilf could go too for a few weeks, until Tom Samson had another shepherd.

It was odd how even Annette called her husband who was fourteen years older than herself 'Squire'. Really it was an endearment which he liked, he hated his name Montague or Monty, so 'Squire' he remained.

Nailus and Kate took the widowed Jane into their cottage leaving the one next door empty for a new shepherd.

Wilf and Gwen took a flock of lambs to the Summer sale and Tom followed in his trap. The market at Oathill, about five miles away, was really a field of hurdled pens, used in August for lamb sales. The field lay next to the small cattle market. Here the market men with crow bars made pens to hold ten or fifteen lambs. The pens were in rows wide enough apart for the auctioneer to ride in a farm waggon.

Here was the moving rostrum for he and his clerk to sell from.

Bowler-hatted and breeched himself, the auctioneer who was also a farmer, used a short cane as a hammer as he sold the lambs. Thousands of lambs in a few hours. These were trucked at Oathill Station for all parts of the country.

"Reminds me of Wales, Wilf," Gwen said as they drove their bunch through the gate. After the sale Wilf and Gwen sat with drivers and farmers eating bread and cheese on the grass. Tom Samson came to take them home in his trap.

"I've just seen a likely shepherd," he said. "He lives about two miles from here, his employer is going out of sheep, and George Barnes says that he doesn't like working with horses or the arable."

Wilf looked at Tom with a sort of look that he and Gwen would like to be shepherds for him for a while.

"I hope he is reliable, Sir," Wilf said. "You have a good flock, you know."

"Yes, that's important, Wilf," Tom replied, "but George says that he has known Nailus for years and I'll ask him. Nailus will be particular about his neighbour."

Wilf and Gwen rounded up the flock every morning. Wilf held the sheep while Gwen clipped the soiled wool from around their tails and poured maggot water on the bunches of maggots. ('Gentles', Nailus called them.)

Squire Mathison rode up the hill with Tom on these summer mornings, pleased that his two workers from the Manor were able to fill a gap in Tom's farming plan.

After consultation with Nailus Tom decided to engage George Barnes.

"I'm afraid my new shepherd won't be available until Michaelmas, Squire," Tom said, adding, "I hope Wilf and Gwen can manage until then or should I say that you can spare them."

Squire Mathison sat on his horse on the brow of the hill,

proud of the way Tom farmed, proud of Wilf and the ways that Annette had instilled into Gwen.

"Don't worry, Tom," he said. "We will manage."

It was a kind of blessing in disguise that Wilf and Gwen were thrown together in this way. Every night they sat by Benedict's Pool when the weather was fine and in Annette's kitchen they had supper together.

Gwen had promised to marry Wilf, but had not named the day. Here among the sheep they talked of a home and furniture, a possible family.

The future seemed rosy.

Wilf said, "When a cottage is empty in the village, will you marry me, Gwen?"

"Yes," Gwen said, "sure I will."

When Michaelmas came George Barnes was ready to move into the next door cottage to Nailus. Taking two horses and a waggon the seven miles to George's cottage, Nailus and Wilf set out early.

"Decent fella George is," Nailus said to Wilf, as they walked beside the horses. "Goodish shepherd."

Wilf nodded, and said, "Is he a young man, Nailus, around my age?"

Nailus laughed and spoke louder as the waggon wheels passed over some rough stones.

"Oi, he was one time a day. Let me see, he's about fifty-nine, and his second wife got a youngster of about eleven. It ull be nice to have a young boy next door, like old times when Garnet's two was at home."

The empty waggon jolted over the cobbled streets of Oathill and they took the lane to Barnes' cottage.

George Barnes and Wilf carried the furniture, Ruth, George's wife, handled the lighter boxes. Nailus stood on the waggon and stacked sideboard, kitchen table, mangle, bedsteads, packing the awkward things with pillows and bolsters.

"We'll have the outside effects on the tailboard. No doubt

thee hast got a fowl pen and a feow hens and a bag or two of taters.''

"Nailus, come and have a last cup of tea in our cottage before we leave," Ruth called from the doorway. They drank their tea in the passage. Everything was loaded except a skep of bees in the garden.

Nailus looked dubiously at these and said, "Thee bisn't a gwain to take them warm-assed craters, be ya, George?"

George and Ruth laughed, even young Albert laughed, because they knew that George had packed them in safe the night before and even if the day was sunny they would travel safely to Samson's farm.

"Shan't touch um," Nailus said. "Never did trust um." So Wilf and George put the hive on the tailboard of the waggon, and roped the load.

George looked at the team, looked at the load, locked the cottage door and took the key to the farmer. He turned to Nailus and said, "Dids't thee walk yer this morning? 'Cos we be a gwain to ride. Albert, get on that trace horse."

"He's a young one," Nailus said.

"And so's Albert," George replied.

The moving family, a familiar sight at Michaelmas, passed through Oathill, Albert on the trace horse, proud as Lucifer, Nailus said, as he drove the filler with the rope reins.

George sat at the front of the waggon with him while Ruth sat in the middle on a chair between the beds holding Shep the sheep dog. When the waggon passed over the loose stones the hens cackled and Ruth was anxious about her crocks in the wicker hamper.

Back at Netherstone by mid-afternoon, the furniture un-loaded, the hens' pen up, and the beehive still closed up under the plum tree, George looked at the empty pig sty. "Didn't your brother keep a pig, Nailus?" he said.

"No, we kept one between us in my sty, useful, unt he?"

Before Garnet's tragic death he had increased Tom Samson's

flock of sheep. In fact, there were now double the number of ewes there had been—on the farm. The sheep had been free from liver fluke and Garnet's skilful handling and feeding had resulted in a good fall of lambs.

Tom Samson decided to keep the best ewe lambs for breeding and further increase his flock.

When George Barnes arrived it was the time to turn the rams with the ewes for Spring lambing.

George settled in quite well at first. His wife liked the cottage and there was just one thing missing, land to keep a few sheep and hens and pigs of his own. Where he had lived before it was a cottage on the edge of a common with grazing rights.

The rams were turned out and raddled with red paste on their breasts to mark each ewe which had been served.

Tom Samson rode round and met George as he came down the hill with his dog Shep.

"How are the tups working, George? I hope the one I bought at Barton Fair is a stockgetter."

Tom looked across the field and saw the ewes' backs marked red with raddle as he spoke to his shepherd.

George, quite used to this sort of question from a farmer any Autumn, replied, "They be doing their work, Gaffer. I've just given um a bit of corn to keep them in good fettle over the Winter. And every morning I recon to give um some corn." George scraped the ground with his crook as if drawing patterns in the turf as he continued nervously:

"Gaffer, you knows that little paddock at the back of our houses where the rams have been all summer. It's about three acres, unt it?"

"Of course, George," Tom replied. "It's called Sally's Piece. What about it?"

George looked at the farmer as he sat astride his horse and plucked up courage to say, "Will you rent it to me, please? I'd like to keep a few ewes of my own and the missus a few hens and a pig or two."

Tom had known this practice of letting a worker have a little land to give him an interest in his job, and something to occupy his spare time after tea.

"Yes, George, I'll do that. We will settle about the rent later."

So George and Ruth and Albert Barnes had a little holding at their back door.

Nailus was dubious about it and told his wife and sister-in-law that sometimes it encourages a man to mix the sugar with the sand.

"What I mean," he said to them over his supper, "is that some men don't know what's their own. Mind ya," he added, "I reckon George is as honest as the day is long. Well, he used to be years ago, but I can't help thinking of the temptation of putting Samson's lambs along of his, that's it."

Aaron Hicks with a village lad

The new reaper

A steam threshing gang rest awhile

The Sunday dig

Annette

Asparagus tied by the wife of a
small holder

Squire Mathison

Pitching and loading the hay

Bait time among the corn

The Rev. Cuthbert going to market

Village folk dressed for the outing

A carter's cart in Netherstone

Steam cultivating

Two young horses

The old village shop

Market gardeners and their wives in the Vale of Evesham

Gwen from Brecon

10

The Major's Move

MAJOR FORBROOKE SINCE LEAVING THE SERVICE HAD been a prominent man on the hunting field. His men Lewes, the stud groom, and Sep, in a short time had built up a stud of horses which any man would be proud to own.

Lewes often talked long and knowledgeably to his employer. He said that the Point-to-Point horses had improved out of all knowledge.

"You know, Sir, we have used some of the best racing stallions in the country on our brood mares and it seems a pity that with such horses we can't compete in higher events, the big meetings."

"Funny thing, Lewes, that's my ambition and before long with the help of you and Sep I hope to race my horses in classic events."

Rosemary Ransome was a frequent guest to the Grange. Adrian, the Major, was so fond of her that he now got jealous if the Vicar called.

"Damn it," he said to Lewes. "He seems to smell when Rosemary makes tea at four o'clock. Got some excuse or other, parish magazine or the stove smokes in the church."

So time passed and Rosemary's radiance, her interest in horses drew her and Adrian together.

Out of the blue one November evening as they sat on the sofa watching and listening to the burning logs in the grate, Adrian proposed marriage.

Rosemary blushed a little saying, "I'll think about it, Adrian."

Rosemary had already thought about it, so when they met a couple of days later she said she would marry him, but if she did, could they get away from Netherstone? "Somewhere," she said, "where we are not known and please, Adrian," she said, "I don't want Bob Cuthbert to marry us."

Adrian was delighted to know that at last he had his bride at a time when he and she could devote a lot of time just being together.

"Yes, Rosemary, we will go from here. Monty Mathison has always wanted this place to add to his estate. Where would you like to go to live, Rosemary, my dear? You must choose a place where you would like."

Rosemary pursed her lips, threw back her hair, and put her arm around Adrian saying near Newbury.

Adrian gasped out, "You are not saying that just for me, are you? Because that's where I would choose to train the horses."

Rosemary giggled as she saw the thoughtful look on the Major's face.

"Well," she said, "I'd be happy there with you."

Adrian was not a man to waste his time, but soon found a farm with horse boxes, a nice ivy-covered gabled house and garden on the Berkshire Down, together they arranged to marry at the village church where they were going.

Squire Mathison bought the Grange.

The Major, Rosemary, Lewes and Sep left Netherstone. Just Monty, the Squire, Annette, Tom and Sarah Samson went to the wedding.

The Vicar Rev Cuthbert refused the invitation. It seemed that other people's lives just fell in place, but Bob Cuthbert must lead a lonely life. There had always been a forlorn hope that Rosemary would marry him. He often thought how much younger he was than the Major, but when Rosemary made her choice it was the Major who became the bridegroom.

In the departure of the four from the Parish of Netherstone the Vicar was hurt; he lost a possible partner in marriage, he lost his churchwarden. As for Sep and Lewes, Bob Cuthbert was not really interested. He sat all day in his study when the four guests who went to the wedding had left on the early train for Berkshire, he sat without food. His life was sad, the only relatives he had were his aged mother up in Yorkshire, and Aunt Hannah who kept house for him.

But the services in church went unabated, Widow Prew played the organ on the Sunday, Tom Samson, Sarah, the Badgers, Annette, the Squire, Nailus and George Barnes and his wife Ruth were at church.

Hannah in her uncouth way, was a comfort to him; she kept the house tidy and did his plain cooking.

The Major's hurried move from Netherstone could be attributed to Rosemary. Not that Rosemary pushed him from the place which he thought would be his home for the rest of his life. No, it was not like that, but when he and Rosemary Ransome who had so recently been widowed found that life together would be so good for them both, their minds were as one—they agreed that Netherstone was not the place to begin their married life. There is no doubt that Rosemary, knowing the Vicar's affection towards her, had a twinge of sympathy for him.

Was Robert Cuthbert ever to find a partner for life?

He wondered all that day of Adrian and Rosemary's wedding why no one wanted to marry him; he thought of Gwen, so different from Rosemary, and yet he could love her. Gwen was the sort of girl who could go anywhere; she was as much at home with the Bishop when he came as with the man who swept the road.

But Gwen's path was plainly marked; there was no doubt now that she and Wilf were meant for each other.

Netherstone would miss the people from the Grange; Rosemary's gaiety left a gap at the hunt and the social life of the village.

Squire Mathison and Annette would keep the people in harmony if possible, but were anxious about their Vicar. His attitude had changed, in fact some thought him over critical of ordinary folk.

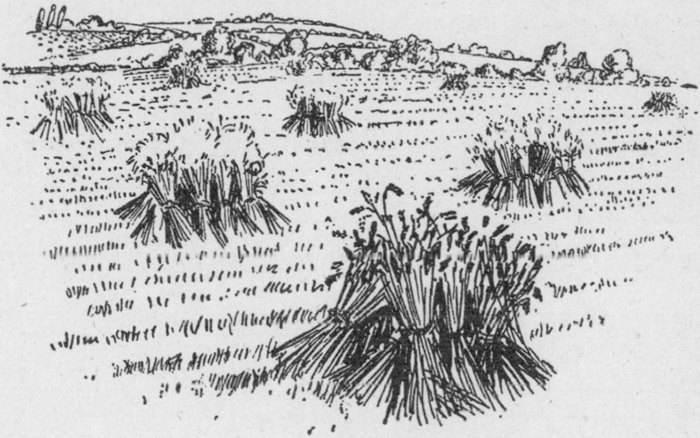

II

Tom Samson's Extra Acres

SQUIRE MATHISON BOUGHT THE MAJOR'S PLACE TO tidy up his estate into a ring fence. There were parts of the Grange Farm where the grass fields squeezed in between Mathison land rented by Tom Samson. "You can manage an extra eighty acres, Tom," Monty Mathison said when the Major left. "£80 a year and a decent house."

Tom and Sarah thought a lot about this proposition. Tom knew that if the plough was put into the grassland rich with horses, corn would grow hedge high for a few years. The stocking of Forbrooke hunters had given the turf a coat of manure which when ploughed in would grow bumper crops.

Tom and the Squire came to an agreement whereby if Tom took the Grange, Wilf and Gwen could live there when they married and Wilf would work for Tom, just helping Aaron Hicks with the pheasants in the rearing season.

"Two more horses we want now," Nailus's voice rang from the stable manger, "and no doubt young Wilf can plough some of the Grange land."

Tom Samson sat on the seat inside the stable and told Nailus to sit on the corn bin for a few minutes while he told him his plans.

"I'm going to Stow Fair to buy two horses, and you, Nailus, I want to teach young Wilf to plough."

Nailus was delighted to have someone who could be called under carter.

Wilf was anxious to marry Gwen and knew that the wedding would be at Brecon.

So one morning in the Spring the couple set off for the Chapel near Brecon where Gwen's parents worshipped. Gwen's mother had recently died, so Mr Owen made it a quiet wedding out of respect for his late wife.

The Samsons went, representing Annette and Monty, and the new Mr and Mrs Cob were installed at the Grange.

Nailus fancied himself as he passed on the mysteries of ploughing turf to Wilf.

"Don't get too dip," he said. "Drop your furrows flatter than usual to bury the grass."

So Wilf whistled and sang behind a pair of roan shire horses. Bounce and Bowler. His furrows were straight after a few days' practice and soon the Grange Farm was transformed from a grassy holding covered with hillocks of horse manure to the rich brown furrows which fell behind Wilf's plough.

Nailus, who ploughed the adjoining field, spent hours squinting up the open furrows cut by Wilf's plough.

"Allus have been the same, Master Samson," he said, "thurs nobody as can't be done without. Wilf ull be ploughing when I be looking up at the daisies in the churchyard."

"Come now, Nailus," his boss replied. "We have not long lost Garnet. You are good for another ten years, specially if you are moderate with Badger's cider."

"Ah, that's what puts 'art in me, Gaffer, certain."

Back at Samson's farm the ewes lambed in perfect weather. George Barnes had plenty of doubles; in fact, few of Samson's ewes dropped single lambs.

In the paddock where George's few ewes grazed they did well and any spare lambs of Samson's were fostered in Ruth Barnes' kitchen, then adopted by George's ewes.

"Every one of his a got doubles, missus," Nailus said one Spring evening after walking around the three-acre paddock, "And what's more, Samson's feed is feeding Barnes' sheep. I never thought he ud stoop to stealing."

Kate told the carter to keep quiet, it was none of his business.

Then young Albert was noticed bringing home baskets of eggs from the Vicarage.

Rev Cuthbert just couldn't understand it that in the Spring when pullets should be in full lay, Hannah brought a mere dozen or so into the dairy.

Nailus met Aaron Hicks at the Cider Mill and together they spoke of the dishonesty of the Barnes family.

Aaron confided in Nailus that Tom Samson had no idea how many lambs he had.

"You see," he said, "when he got his tailing money George Barnes the shepherd was sly and din't count all the tails cut from the lambs. It's true he only got paid so much a score for all the tails he took to Tom, but the twenty-five lambs that were not counted he reckoned on selling to a dealer later on. He could do this together with his own lambs."

Nailus no longer trusted George Barnes; in fact he was hurt to know that the man he recommended to take his brother's place was dishonest. He did no more than pass the time of day with him.

His voice was sad, his eyes were damp with tears when he talked with Aaron, speaking of the days when he and Garnet worked for the Samson's family, of the poaching of Sep.

"Sep was but a buoy," he said, "but George Barnes is robbing our Gaffer right, left and centre. Ruth his missus is mixed up in it too; she steals apples from the orchard—well, she did in the Autumn."

Aaron spoke softly explaining how it had left a lasting impression on him when he just had to shoot at Sep to save his own life.

"Passion, 'tis a terrible thing," Nailus answered as he bought another pint of cider for Aaron, and one for himself.

"You understand my meaning when I say that me and Garnet allus was straight with our Gaffer. We only had the money we earned apart from little extras the Squire gave us at Christmas."

Aaron sighed, then smiled, saying, "I'm so glad Wilf and

Gwen are settled in at the Grange. Now there's a man who can be trusted. Tom Samson's got a good chap to manage that place.''

Nailus was quick to add, "Oi, I taught him how to plough, mind tha' and Annette has missed the Welsh girl at the Manor so Jane, Garnet's widow goes along days and helps, I yerd a whisper that Annette's in the family way. That ull please the Squire, especially if it's a buoy.''

Aaron stared into the fire as Nailus said, "I'd like to see you married man, Aaron.''

These meetings at the Cider Mill became a regular thing for the gamekeeper to look forward to. He seldom went there when Sep lived in the village although Aaron was sorry for Sep in a way. Sorry because he had never been brought up to work like he and Nailus had, brought up to know what was his own.

Tom Samson's extra acres were green with barley. It was a credit to Wilf that his first year at the Grange looked so promising. No small credit to Gwen either, because she was out in the stable in the mornings when the head-lands of the fields were drenched with dew, feeding and grooming Bounce and Bowler ready for Wilf to go to work. It was a foregone conclusion that she would load the waggons at harvest and haymaking from the pitchers, Nailus, Wilf and Tom and the doubtful George Barnes.

Nailus and Aaron missed the Major, the joyful chatter of Rosemary, the steady Lewes, but were glad to see Wilf and Gwen here at the Grange like junior bailiffs.

What a blow to Netherstone Garnet's death had been. Now it was doubled by the dishonest dealing of the Barnes family.

Nailus saw it all, living next door. He saw the dealers of Oathill fetch the eggs, some of Barnes' and a lot of the Vicar's.

Some nights a dressed lamb was collected in a strange cart. A lamb of Samson's killed in his pig sty hung in his cellar, all the waste including the skin burnt in the copper furnace. Nailus was hurt more than if it were his own property.

Luckily as time went on George Barnes realised he had a good job and a good boss. He wanted to stay at Netherstone and see his boy start work there and so he began to go straight again. As Nailus knew, George was basically honest. This was the first time he had been tempted to feather his nest by these mean tricks.

12

Annette Mathison's Son

ON A COLD CRISP WINTER'S MORNING AS NETHERSTONE Church clock struck five, Nailus led his horses from the hoary meadow to the warmth of Tom Samson's stable. Here the powerful shires that would be pulling the plough during the day pulled sweet red clover from the fodder rack.

Nailus halted for a moment outside the stable door, where he stood lantern in hand looking up at the stars. Something different about 'The Hill' this morning he thought as his eyes caught sight of lights glowing through the curtains both downstairs and in Squire Mathison's bedroom.

Leaving his horses to eat their fodder Nailus strolled across the rickyard to the edge of the paddock adjoining 'The Hill'.

The doctor's trap from Oathill stood with its candle lamps still alight and his cob tied to the garden railings.

"Summat unusual this morning," he thought as he walked back to the stable "and this time of day, the village has not stirred as a rule except for me and George Barnes."

Gwen Cob rushed through the yard.

"What's up, Gwen? Thee bist like a cow with the bree breviting about like a blue-assed fly?"

Gwen panted and replied, "'Tis all over, Nailus."

"What's over?" Nailus muttered.

"Mrs Mathison has just given birth to a boy. The doctor's still there having a drink with the Squire, Mary Badger is looking after the baby and the Squire's wife."

"Well I be damned," Nailus shouted to the Welsh girl, "if it unt my birthday too, but the saying is, 'When the apple's ripe it ull fall'."

The news soon spread around the village and Monty Mathison entertained a few of the folk to a drink that evening. Rev Cuthbert and his Aunt Hannah Loosestrife, Tom and Sarah Samson, Wilf and Gwen, the doctor and his wife. Joe Badger had a note delivered to him by young Albert Barnes that after the farm men had rung the bells, they were to have refreshments at 'The Cider Mill' at the Squire's expense.

Squire Mathison added a rider to tell Joe not to let them drink to excess. This was really unnecessary, Joe knowing his customers.

"Young Wilf's been made hell of a fuss of by the folks at the Hall," Nailus said to George the next morning. "Hob nobbing along the Gentry."

George leant on his crook and propped against the stable door said, "'Tis like this yer, Nailus, and allus bin the same since Adam was a buoy. You taught young Wilf to plough, I've showed him a wrinkle or two about how to lamb a ewe, Aaron taught him a bit of gamekeeping. Now he's a Bailee for our Gaffer at the Grange, he's a cut above the likes of we now he's married Gwen. Education," Nailus sighed as he put the collar on one of his plough team. "Still, he's done a smartish job at the Grange, keeps a diary they do say."

"Mind ya, the Grange farm was as poor as Job's heart when the Major keeps his horses there. Horses thick on the ground ruins the pasture, all it grows be mushrooms."

"Oi, horses muck for mushrooms, and I be partial to um."

That Winter Annette's parents spent at the Hall, bringing with them a nurse from London.

"Her's a tidy piece," Nailus told Kate one evening when he had met her in the road pushing the bassinet with Edward Mathison out for an airing.

"Oi, hair as black as the raven's wing, upstanding wench."

Kate looked at her husband and saw that he still had a twinkle in his eye.

"You know, Nailus," she said, "the way you talk of women

sounds more like as if you were judging a cart horse. Still, I agree Margaret the nursemaid is a sight for sore eyes, a beautiful girl. Have a cup of tea, Nailus, and think of me a bit more."

Nailus put his rough horny hand on Kate's shoulder and whispered, "If I could see my time over again, I'd marry the same 'ooman. I beunt complaining."

The routine at Netherstone went on and planting and reaping, grazing and mowing came as sure as the bore or the high spring tides flooded the Severn meadows. As certain as the elvers or young eels came up that same river, small fry from the spawn from a distant sea.

Young Edward Mathison grew in the springtime with the same certainty as George Barnes' lambs. Rev Cuthbert christened the Squire's son in Netherstone Church. Annette became her usual self again, a kindly young Lady Bountiful of the village, always at hand to help the humble labourer's wife, to be a stay for the Vicar in church affairs while Margaret looked after Edward.

13

Wilf Cob Farms Netherstone

On Lady Day when the Squire's son was just over a year old, his father decided that Tom Samson should be his partner to farm the parish. Tom had farmed Mathison's land well and Wilf had proved himself at the Grange.

The agreement was drawn up that whereas Monty Mathison owned all the land and houses in the village, Tom Samson would be his partner. This would give Mathison and Samson added incentive to make the best of the fertile land, allowing Tom to have equal rights in the woods, and all labour would be available where and when needed.

Tom and Monty thought it in their best interests to make Wilf Cob Bailiff of the estate.

From now on the Mathisons would be more involved in the cropping and cultivation of the land and the Samsons would have a say in the future of the woods, pheasant rearing, etc., and, most important of all, the Mathisons would be more willing to put capital into the estate knowing that their partner would be wise in its use.

"A most sensible arrangement," the Vicar said when he heard. "I'm sure the parish will be more of a family than ever before."

Wilf and Gwen were pleased with the news. Wilf did mention to the partners that if the land was to be farmed to produce its maximum crops, he would need some more labour.

"So it's Mathison and Samson we be working for," Nailus told George, "and young Wilf's a gwain to give the orders."

"What do you think of the change, Master Cuthbert?"
Nailus asked the Netherstone parson.

"Well, you know, Nailus, changes will come to all of us. I
think of you and your brother Garnet often you know. I think
of trees as old familiar friends—we cannot bear to lose them and
every one that falls reminds us of the days that are no more.
Reminds us of

> Those who once gave promise
> Of fruit for manhood's prime
> Have passed from us for ever
> Gone before their time."

"But, Master Cuthbert, our Garnet was passed before his
prime."

"Ah," the Vicar replied. "It's the Silent Reaper. Others will
fill our places."

On Saturday when Wilf first paid all the men on the Netherstone estate, he told them that he knew that they would work
for him as loyally as a team as they had always done. Like an
army officer he looked for gaps in the ranks. "Albert can handle
horses now, Master Cob," George spoke up. "And we can do
with the extra coppers."

Wilf said, "Yes, Albert can have a permanent place in
Netherstone farms now, and I can find more regular work for the
womenfolk."

Gwen kept an account of the work done on the estate and
money paid for wages, her diary gave a word picture of the state
of crops and the weather. For instance, August 3rd, when the
men all helped at harvest carrying 'clover'. And, 'August 4th,
Making staddles for corn ricks, staddles of wood faggots over
staddle stones.'

Then throughout the month when three days were spent
hedge cutting it meant that the rains had come.

'August 20th—After some swede turnip hoeing had been

finished. Barley mowing for several days, then mowing docks.'
Presumably it was a wet day.

'August 26th—Barley cocking.' That's putting the mown
barley into little ricks in the field.

'August 28th—Barley carrying to the ricks. Finished the
barley.'

For nine days Nailus, George, Aaron and Wilf were ricking
the wheat. Tom Samson tied his horse to the gate and worked
part of the day.

The second week in September they were bagging a piece of
wheat laid by the storms which the binder would not cut.

'September 28th—Threshing the corn.'

The women were employed in Summer haymaking, raking
clover, pulling weeds, turnip hoeing. Then two days a week,
Jane Bullin went washing first to the Manor, then to Samson's
Farm.

Widow Prew led a lonely life in the cold winds of March,
gathering couch grass, swede cleaning, stone picking. That is to
say picking up the stones on the hill fields which were hauled
by Nailus and Albert to fill in the winter-made wheel ruts by
Benedict's Pool.

George Barnes, whose flock of sheep had been reduced, filled
in time forking out couch grass and burning it. On April 16th,
Gwen put in her diary, 'Nailus all day turning the Muck Bury.'

Wilf then employed two more men who lived at Widow
Prew's cottage, Harry and Bill Stokes.

'May 21st—Throwing up the limekiln.
          Pulling up Crow onions.'

'May 27th—Nailus in the Garden all day keeping out the
cow.'

The cow was an Alderney, one of three kept at the Grange,
the other two being referred to as the horned cow and the
Hereford.

'May 28th—George Barnes killed a giddy welter weighing
$55\frac{1}{2}$ lb. (This would be a welter sheep or castrated ram of over

twelve months old, the cause of Gid being a sort of maggot or grub which attacks the brain so that the sheep runs in circles.)

Gwen's diary records for October 16th—'They put the Old ram to mate with 44 theaves (maiden ewes).'

'October 17th—Put the Ram to mate with 41 ewes.'

So here we see how Shakespeare's maxim was followed by Wilf, an experienced old ram is to couple with the maiden ewe; an inexperienced young ram with the older ewes.

Rev Robert Cuthbert was so pleased with the way Netherstone was forward-looking that he mentioned the new partnership in his parish magazine. His descriptions of life in the village under Netherstone Hill were particularly good, although Bob Cuthbert in the words of Nailus never lapped or wrapped anything up. Taking advantage of his parish magazine, he praised the villagers when praise was due and chastised them when they strayed (as Nailus said) "from the straight and narra." His outspoken remarks about the churchyard are worth noting. 'It has been decided to ban artificial flowers in hideous glass globes which are a terrible disfigurement to our grand churchyard. These horrible eyesores have been the miserable invention of the terrible shark the modern undertaker whose sole idea seems to be to prey upon the feelings of the unhappy victims to run them to unnecessary expense under the impression they are honouring the dead.'

Jane Bullin read this and as the tears streamed down her wrinkled face onto the paper she sobbed out to her sister-in-law Kate:

"Our Garnet, may God rest his soul, used to bring me the first primroses in the springtime. He picked them where they allus grew on the mossy banks of the stream in Netherstone Coppice."

"Ah," Kate replied, "'tis what I've allus bin told that the time a body wants flowers is when they be alive. The Vicar's right the glass bowls don't mean a thing and they look so out of place when the wild flowers be in the hedgerows, when the hawthorn's in blow and the plum trees at the Grange as Wilf has planted show white with flower as pure as the driven snow."

Jane put down the paper adding, "A feow flowers picked from the garden and put in a jam jar don't look amiss. That's what marks the spot where my man lies."

Down at the Cider Mill Nailus and George talking to Harry and Bill Stokes discussed Bob Cuthbert's magazine and agreed that the Vicar had the people of the parish close to his heart. The trouble was, Nailus said, that our parson has lived a life with old Hannah Loosestrife and got her old-fashioned ways. "He unt a keeping up with the times."

Joe Badger the landlord laughed as he turned the wooden tap on and the pale glow of the cider from the trammed barrel flowed into Nailus's quart mug. Nailus always started with a quart; it was his way of letting the other customers know that he was a man with an ample stomach for the wine of the West.

"That's as may be," Mary Badger now joined in the conversation. "I hold with what he says about the flowers in glass vases, but what about his remarks about Good Friday? Here's the words." With this she fingered the pages until she read: " 'Last year's attendance was unsatisfactory, the three hours service in particular. There was one thing which grieved me very much, and that was that all our dear children went away to Netherstone Hill for the day and spent it like a holiday and not a Holy day'."

"Can't blame um," George Barnes butted in. "Three hours is a devilish long time to sit with yer ass on a wooden bench."

"Quiet, George," Mary raised her voice. "Let me finish.

" 'Children have souls as well as grown ups and the more they are treated as grown ups in spiritual things the better. It is one of the Devil's devices to make us think that it does not matter much about children as long as they are children but we ought always to remember that the child is father to the man.

" 'Good Friday is a sad and solemn day and I hope that our children will do better next year'."

Nailus's eyes twinkled as he looked at Mary. "You and me, Mary, knows what it was like when we were young, tater planting all day. I used to carry a peck basket and drop the taters in the trench for our Dad to dig the allotment. Unt Cuthbert ever going to see that a country parish is different from one in the smoke?"

"What dos't myun by the smoke?" Bill Stokes nudged him. "Ast ever been there?"

"Oi, London," Nailus laughed. "Only once though, and I didn't see no tater planting there."

At this point Wilf Cob walked into the Cider Mill. He was excited having just come from the Hill where he had spent some hours with Squire Mathison and Tom Samson.

"Could I have a word with Harry and Bill Stokes?" he said to Joe Badger. "Just a bit of business."

"Harry," Joe called towards the inglenook, "the boss wants a word with you. Go into the front parlour, Master Cob, it's quiet in there."

Harry and Bill went into the next room with Wilf.

"Nothing wrong, I hope," Bill said, looking down his nose.

"Oh just the opposite," Wilf replied. "I've got news for you both." He then explained to the brothers that at long last he had persuaded Mathison and Samson to buy two steam ploughing engines, a plough which ploughed five furrows at once and a cultivator. He said he understood that Harry had driven a steam engine at his last place on a large estate. Harry nodded.

Wilf said that if Harry would instruct Bill how to use an engine that soon the larger fields could be ploughed deep by the steam tackle, and furthermore, that they had been able to rent a large part of the Marquis's estate. This would make them the largest farmers in the West Midlands. "Six thousand acres we shall have."

"I'll drive the engine and show Bill how to," Harry told Wilf, "but we shall want a boy to ride the plough. Albert will do that."

Wilf had seen Albert and the idea thrilled him.

Back in the bar Aaron had joined George and Nailus and as Wilf left, an excited young Bailiff, Mathison and Samson's men sat speechless for a time. The only noises being the fizz of the barrel tap when Joe drew a pint of drink and the belches of Nailus as he emptied his crock pot.

Then Nailus spoke to George, George's face was mischievous. He knew that the new pattern of Netherstone farming would not affect him a lot, but he also knew that Nailus's work would be altered. Altered in a way where more corn would be planted by him, and his team of horses would be secondary to the steam engines.

"Them Black 'Orses be gwain to be a damn nuisance to me, ye know, George," he said, then held his little group who just had to listen to his opinion of 'Black 'Orses' or steam engines.

"'Tis like this yer," he said. "We have had um yer years ago, when Tom Samson's father was alive. They ploughs the furrow deep and wide, and I had the job hauling water to the engines with a pair of 'orses on the water cart. It unt so bad the first time over with the plough, because it's easy to take the water barrel along the head-land where the stubble or grassland lies undisturbed like, then they plough the head-land and put one engine at each end of the field and use the scuffle [cultivator] to stir up and break the furrows. The one engine pulls the cable winding in the drums, the other pays out the cable from his drum, the buoy rides the cultivator."

Aaron relit his pipe and said, "Well, what the steam tackle ploughs and cultivates, you won't have to, Nailus."

"That's just where you be mistook, Aaron, my buoy. The scuffle leaves big clats [clods] of clay as big as 'osses' yuds and me and my 'osses ull have the caper of getting the ground down fine, fit to plant. Oi, I know it ull be 'Put the roller over the fallow, Nailus' and I'll be no more than a clod hopper. No, my buoy, I beunt relishing the coming of the Iron 'Osses to our place, we was going on comfortable afore."

Nailus turned to George adding, "What bist thee a grinning at like a Cheshire cat?"

George patted Nailus on the shoulder saying, "Thy shoulders be broad but it unt thy worry but Wilf and the Gaffer's over us."

All the time Joe Badger was listening and remembering the trouble there was when the new binder came. Joe knew that Nailus wanted no changes in farming and remembered Nailus' usual saying, "That the work allus was done years ago."

"I suppose you chaps realise that now our employers have taken over so much more land that I shall have more woodland to look after," Aaron Hicks commented. "I know the bulk of it is known as 'The Waste' and is unsuitable for pheasant shooting, but nevertheless it will be rough shoot that I shall have the care of."

Nailus looked wildly at all the men in the Mill and raised his voice and thumped his stick on the flagstone floor as he said:

"It's like a job in the town walking the woods in breeches and gaiters. I be the one who ull suffer in my feet and legs. Let's have another pint, Joe. Then perhaps I shall sleep tonight."

I suppose the one person in the Cider Mill that night who was sorry for the ploughman was Mary Badger, the landlord's wife.

She thought how right he was in his estimation of the changes, and how the coming of steam to Samson's Farm would affect him. How can I cheer the old chap up? She racked her brains. Then Mary remembered that Rev Cuthbert had called the week before and asked her if she would like to go to Bournemouth on the Choir outing.

"Would you like a day in Bournemouth, Nailus, at the sea?" Mary asked him. "It's the choir outing and the Vicar asked me to tell my customers that they would be welcome to come."

"The sea," Nailus said. "I a never sin the sea. Oi, I'll come, damned if I won't! How be us a going? By train, I suppose."

"Oi, steam engine," George chafed him with this untimely remark.

"Shut thee rattle, George, I be gwain to the sea. They tells me thurs hozone there good for the lungs."

"Right," Mary said amid the laughter in the bar. "You and Kate can sit by me. I believe the Vicar is reserving some compartments in the train. George and Ruth are coming—well, that's what Ruth has promised."

George raised his eyebrows and agreed that if Ruth wanted an outing he was game to come.

14

The Outing

THE EXCURSION TRAIN FROM OATHILL STARTED EARLY
that July morning when the Vicar of Netherstone shepherded his
flock to the station. The Squire and Tom Samson arranged for
ponies and traps, governess carts, to leave the village before
dawn.

Nailus drove Joe Badger's spring cart with Mary, Kate and
George, Ruth and Jane. Joe stayed at home to keep the Cider
Mill open.

As the party of thirty-five villagers stepped into the reserved
compartment, the sun was just showing a golden line along the
ridge of hills to the east.

"It's a gwain to be a real haymaker to-day, Vicar. The sun
went down red to bed last night and the morning dew drenched
my boots when I got Master Badger's pony from the paddock
early on." Nailus was speaking in his usual prophetic way, a
way now familiar to Rev Cuthbert.

"Quite, quite, I think we shall have it warm. Now you and
George, I'm sure, can be trusted not to have too much beer
to-day. Everything in moderation, don't you agree?"

The Vicar's hint to Tom Samson's old carter was taken kindly
as he replied:

"Oh no, Master Cuthbert, we buent the sort of folks as
abuses themselves."

As the train left the station with the Squire, the Vicar,
Annette and Mr and Mrs Samson sat in the carriage accompanied by
Gwen and Wilf. The other parishioners mingled together, the
choir boys being under the care of Aaron Hicks.

Nailus farmed all morning from the carriage window and his conversation got Kate and Jane annoyed after a while. You see, this was Nailus's one opportunity of criticising the way the land was being worked.

"Ah," he chuckled to George, "that hay rick's askew, got the props to keep him from falling. Good bit of ploughing in the next field though." "Only just getting the cows in yon." He turned to Kate. "Thurs a afternoon sort of fella, he should have milked be now."

Kate looked at Jane and saw the cowman driving his herd to the buildings. Kate said, "Now, Nailus, you know what our parson said about the beer. If you keep talking it will take a lot to slake your thirst."

George was more interested in the Downland sheep. He noticed ewes badly shorn and said that his father always said that sheep that were sheared uneven looked just the same as ones done tidy in a month's time.

"Partridge nests!" Nailus exclaimed as the train passed a hay field cleared and ricked.

Mary Badger was amazed and inquired of Kate how Nailus was blessed with such eyesight.

Nailus answered and George laughed as they both said, "Partridge nests be little tussocks of grass that the mower has missed."

"Now sometimes," said Nailus, "'tis done a purpose to save a clutch of eggs being hatched by the hen bird, but in general, 'tis bad workmanship, the mower has driven his horses wide of the swath and missed a bit."

Passing the Oxford colleges Nailus reached for his frail basket off the luggage rack and he and George unwrapped their bread and cheese and drank from their cider bottles.

"Well," Jane said, "can't that wait a bit? 'Tis only six o'clock."

Nailus wiped his whiskery mouth, looked at the telegraph poles passing and as the train rocked on its iron road he said in a whisper, "Me and George only had a dew bit this morning, just a morsel when the dew lay on the grass—no proper breakfast."

When the frail basket was back in its place on the rack Nailus fell asleep, snoring with his lower lip dropped showing what George the shepherd said was a mouth like a broken-mouthed ewe, an old ewe with half her teeth gone.

Near Southampton George saw two steam engines in a big field, one under each hedge and a young chap riding the plough as the cable pulled him across the field. The cable rope was tight in front of the plough and the engine which pulled with the revolving drum under her boiler was puffing out clouds of smoke and steam. The other engine idled as she let the slack rope cable run from her reel drum.

"Shall we wake him?" George asked Kate. Kate winked her eye in approval.

"Look ya, Nailus, Black 'Osses." George nudged the carter awake.

"Well, damn it all," Nailus said as the train slowed and stopped at a signal. "I bo come yer to-day to get away from them inventions of the Devil," and he looked the other way.

Soon the train was running close to the sea at Southampton. This gave the Vicar chance to look at the ships in Southampton water with his telescope. The choir boys were excited in Aaron's compartment when they saw the boats, big and small, sailing close inshore.

Nailus exclaimed that "Allus I bin told the sea is blue! Now thur it is just like a green medda in the spring time and the waves reminds me of ripples in the standing corn, white as milk on the top." Then he added, "Thurs a hell of a lot of room out there among the ships. America the Parson says they comes from to here, I'd relish a ride over the waves, what says you, missus?"

Kate pursed her lips, looked at Jane and Mary and said, "Well, if it's not too rough at Bournemouth."

At Bournemouth, Nailus and George were anxious to cool their feet in the sea, so on the sands they took off their hob-nailed boots, tied their leather laces together and slung them over their shoulder. With turned up corduroy trousers the two men let the little waves lap over their feet.

"A ya seen the Vicar with Gwen and Wilf?" George shouted to make his voice heard above the groan of the sea.

"Where is he?" Jane called back from the sands where she sat with Kate.

"Aaron and buoys says they be in the bathing machine," George replied, and taking another look said, "They looks more like shepherds' huts we uses for lambing."

"Yer, George," Ruth called from the beach. "Don't make a fool of yourself. They be gone to the huts to change into their costumes."

The wooden huts on wheels were at the water edge and soon the Vicar, Wilf and Gwen came out of the three huts they had hired and were swimming in the sea.

Nailus stood back and watched three of the party swimming like fish through the waves.

"Looks to me more like great eels, they be as black as the ace of spades," he said. Then he ran from the water.

Two of the choir boys laughed as Nailus called them to the water's edge where he showed them a crab that he found under a pebble.

"He's like one a them great toads as I have seen round Benedict's Pool, but them pinchers keeps opening and shutting like a dog with teeth. I buen't a gwain in again 'cos I recons he might take a fancy to one a my toes."

On the beach Nailus viewed the scene, took another swig of cider from his bottle, sitting down by Kate who was eating plum cake with the other women.

"Roll up, Roll up, the boat leaves for Swanage in twenty minutes," a navy blue jerseyed seaman called from the entrance to the pier.

By now the Vicar, Wilf and Gwen were dressed and had come from what George had called the shepherd huts.

"Would any of you good folk like a trip to Swanage at my expense?" he said.

Hearing this about half of the party followed Bob Cuthbert to the end of the pier. Here they boarded the steamer which followed the coast to Swanage. Nailus and George just could not take their eyes from the expanse of sea to the south and the Isle of Wight to the east.

"What I like about it, George," Nailus said at last, "thurs enough water for everyone."

"What's over that a road, Vicar?" he added.

"France," Rev Cuthbert replied. "About a hundred miles off, I suppose."

Then, whispering to George so that the other passengers couldn't hear, Nailus told him that France is "the place where they eats frogs, so I be told in the pub."

Back at the pier a young man in a white jacket was calling "A good dinner for eightpence." Nailus and George called the women folk into the restaurant.

"Sit yourselves down, the beef looks morelsh."

"Never had me fittle over the sea afore," Nailus said, as he listened to the waves beating against the pier.

The food was good but when the first course was finished, before the plum pie came round, Nailus raised his plate to his lips and noisily drank the gravy.

"Lors, just look at my man!" Kate exclaimed. "I be mortically ashamed of him."

"Don't thee think I be gwain to waste that liquor, that's the best of the beef and I be paying for it." Nailus was riled as he answered to his wife.

After dinner Aaron showed the choir boys the parish church, then bought them lemonade from a stall on the promenade, and all too soon thirty-five folk of Netherstone were at the station.

On the platform the village folk talked of what they had seen.

Aaron was impressed by the band on the pier, where he had sat in deck chairs with the choir boys and with the Squire, Annette, Tom and Sarah Samson.

Kate did say to Jane and Mary how glad she was that they had a compartment to themselves with Nailus and George and Kath. You see Nailus's manners were learnt in the spit and sawdust of the Cider Mill and not fit for the company of gentle folk.

"I be gwain to take my jacket off," Nailus announced in the hot railway compartment and as the beads of perspiration trickled down her cheeks Jane took off her hat and the other ladies followed suit.

"Dost recon it's proper," George inquired, "to behave like this?"

"I'll warrant the Parson a got his dog collar off by now," was Nailus's opinion.

And so the outing proceeded to Oathill where the horses waited to take the Netherstone choir and friends back home.

In the parish magazine the Vicar wrote an account of the day at Bournemouth:

The Choir outing on 18 July. At 3 a.m. or thereabouts the party of 35 in number including the Vicar and The Wardens, their ladies, the choir boys started for Oathill where by the Excursion train leaving Oathill at 4, they proceeded to Bournemouth in reserved compartments. The sun shone gloriously and it was quite evident from the first the weather was going to be Royal. Passing through Oxford and Basingstoke the train dashed down to Southampton where a glimpse was had of ships.

Then once again through the New Forest cool and shady till at last at 9.25. Bournemouth was reached, the train being only a few minutes late.

The party was then escorted by some friends of the Vicar to the entrance of the Gardens and divided, some going to the Pier, others to the sands.

Later the Vicar took half of our number by steamer to Swanage.

Those on the Pier heard Mr Godfrey's magnificent Band. Sea bathing was indulged in.

At 5 p.m. those that went to Evensong at St Peter's heard psalms and canticles sung in Gregorian settings.

The boys, we were pleased to notice, took a great interest in the Church while the intelligent Verger explained everything to us most carefully.

Then climbing on top of a headland we were soon inhaling the beautiful air of that lofty elevation.

Some of our members took the opportunity to have a drive four in hand along the whole length of the Promenade.

The excellent behaviour of the boys showed that they are capable of conducting themselves in a manner worthy of the occasion.

Then with lingering steps we made towards the Central Station where at 8.5 p.m. we embarked for home.

The journey was hot and most of the gentlemen dispensed with their coats and ladies with their hats. Oathill was reached 1.30 a.m., 10 minutes late, when a drive home by traps and other vehicles in the fresh morning air was refreshing.

15

The Stocking of Bevington Waste

THE CAST OR YIELD OF CORN AT NETHERSTONE increased with the introduction of steam tackle by Mathison and Samson. For years Nailus and Wilf had scratched the top six inches of soil with their iron Ransome plough. They used the Worcestershire nine-legged cultivator or scuffle to clean the land to produce a mould [tilth] to plant the corn. Often with three horses abreast, the duckfoot drags were pulled by the team across the furrow to produce a finer seed bed, possible with this heavy type of harrow with ducks feet tines.

Now things had changed. The Partners with the huge acreage of land in neighbouring parishes, each with a bailiff on each farm, sent their steam ploughs to the fields where the Winter storm water lay on a pan of clay unable to drain and raked ruthlessly at the subsoil and so with lime and soot and farmyard manure, the whole area became enriched.

This process took years to bear fruit. Some hedges around the smaller fields were grubbed up to make way for the new giants of cultivation.

It was a pleasant sight on a blistering hot July day to watch Harry and Bill Stokes with their engines on opposite head-lands hissing steam and smoke, with young Albert riding the five-furrow plough backwards and forward pulled by the cable.

Late into the evening they worked. This was so alien to Nailus whose team were tired by late afternoon. He and George stood one such evening against a field gate and watched the heavy plough turn over the clover sward on sun-baked land, where the chauns or cracks were deep enough to swallow a walking stick.

George nudged Nailus as the plough turned over the hard, almost rock-like soil showing the bulbous roots of clover. Clover which had sent its feelers down deep to find moisture that dry summer.

"Dost recon four hosses in line would turn over one furrow afore the rain has softened the top soil a morsel, you?" George asked the old ploughman in a half sarcastic way.

Nailus shook his head as he replied, "No, George buoy, my plough share just udn't tackle that sort of going, not if six horses were hitched on the beam."

Aaron on his evening round joined the men at the gate.

"Tidy job they are making of the ley and over in the next field the wheat looks kind where the steam tackle worked last year."

"Oi, that's true," Nailus replied, "and you can't go beyond the truth."

Aaron's eyes followed Albert on the plough for several minutes. George asked, "What's got on thee mind, Aaron? Be the pheasants a growing well? No doubt you have lost a feow partridges down these deep channels in the ground. Bound to, I recon."

"No, it's not that, George, but I've heard news to-day which will surprise the whole district. You know that big piece of rough cover stretching from the main road to the railway line and most of it in fact in the next parish?"

"Oi, Bevington Waste you myuns," Nailus answered. "What about it? All that I know is it's that damn thick of bramble thorn and stunted trees it ud be difficult to drive a bull through it."

Aaron looked towards the men and said, "Mathison and Samson are going to stock it up and plant it with corn."

Nailus and George laughed at the idea. Aaron was not amused, knowing that the Waste was good cover for a rough shoot and the local pack of foxhound always found a fox there when they met at the Marquis' place.

"Well, that's the plan," Aaron replied, "and a very well-known land agent, an expert in drainage and land clearance, has been engaged to tackle the job."

"Master Grove from Oathill, I suppose." Nailus's guess was right. Aaron nodded, "Yes, that's him."

Bevington was 414½ acres. The challenge to clear this land, drain it and produce corn was one which, although large in extent, to Mr Grove was a contract which he was used to, having diverted rivers and drained thousands of acres of useless land. The owner of the land, the Marquis, was pleased that Squire Mathison with the co-operation of his partner Tom Samson was so eager to produce corn from a wilderness of thorn.

Mr Grove's men worked like an Army. Five hundred of them came by special train to Oathill Station; they hailed from almost every county in Britain. It seemed apparent to the folk of Netherstone that Mr Grove was taking advantage of the Government scheme for land drainage and improvement. Four million pounds had been authorised by the Treasury for such schemes some years before.

Let us relive the scene on that day when the nineteenth century was in its last quarter or nearly so, and five hundred strong men dressed in corduroy breeches, strong cord jackets, with strong arms and strong hearts left the train at Oathill Station.

Mr Grove, known to one and all as the General, marched them first to Oathill Town Hall, then walking in front of his Army moved up High Street to attack the Waste.

The General was a powerful, disciplined man. The men followed with spades, mattocks and axes at the slope like rifles on their broad shoulders.

Harry and Bill Stokes with young Arthur were at Bevington Waste with the two steam engines. Nailus hauled coal with a muck cart from Oathill Station, in fact he had been hauling coal for some time before the Army arrived.

Albert was not needed to ride a plough at the early stage so he was told by Wilf to take two horses and the water cart to supply the Black 'Osses with water. He pumped it by hand from the nearest pond.

If you imagine an army of five hundred men, it soon becomes clear that foremen are needed to work under the General to operate the scheme smoothly. Old Boots of the Gardeners Square at Oathill recruited men no one knew from where. Eli who became a public house landlord was one such man and another 'Hellfire Jack' of Kersoe, a noted woodman.

As Mr Mathison, Tom Samson and Wilf arrived on the scene the operations had just begun.

The whole area from Bevington to Lench was on a part of the Wyre Forest. It was covered with squat-topped oak trees looking as if they had been pollarded, useless for timber, with a thick undergrowth of brush and hawthorn mixed with sloe-covered blackthorn bushes.

Nailus was right, you couldn't drive a bull through the jungle of growth.

Squire Mathison took a spade and sampled the soil; soil so different from Netherstone. Here was light, friable, mould full of the rotted vegetation of centuries, a gold mine in agricultural terms.

"Once it's cleared," Tom told the Squire, "we will show the people of this district how to grow corn."

And so the operation began with mattocks flying and spades digging through the briars.

"We be yer to deal with the rough stuff," Nailus told Albert as they passed on the Oathill road, Nailus with a load of coal and Albert with a butt or barrel of water.

"Stokes' engine be gwain to pull up some of the bigger oaks after this legion have cut the roots with their mattocks and axes."

Nailus went home in the trap with Albert. In the Cider Mill some of the men from Bevington slaked their thirst at night and told Nailus the terms of their work.

"We get £15 per acre stocked, contract price, but we must leave the land dug one spit deep, spade dug at that, not with forks. Drainage, which will come later, will be £5 per acre drained."

Such was the magnitude of the stocking of Bevington Waste that the Vicar of Netherstone drove over in his trap. He talked with the rough tattooed men of Wales and the Black Country who camped in huts at night, inquired after their families, and anyone in trouble could rely on him and Aunt Hannah Loosestrife for shelter and help at Netherstone Vicarage. Annette, Gwen and Sarah Samson helped to nurse any of the men who were laid up from their work by accident on this somewhat dangerous job of clearing thickly wooded wasteland.

So the mattocks and axes of Mr Grove's Army slew the scrubby trees and stocked the creeping bramble bushes.

Old men on the Alcester road, the Lench road, strolled towards the sound of metal against wood, listened to the creak and crackle of inferior timber. "Many's the time," they said, "we have shot wood pigeons from that pollard oak. They fed on the winter berried ivy, now the steam engines have made its head nod a time or two."

Hellfire Jack and Art stood by while the cable strained from Mathison steam engine. Art called to the old men on the roadside, "Mind yer backs. That there oak anant the road might twist your way."

The old men moved back and stood and stared.

"Tidy yud on that oak I know, 'cos it's many years since I pollarded him with my axe. I be related to Art. Uncle in fact, but then I finished working for the Marquis when I was seventy-five."

His friend turned and said, "Yes, we be both still living in his houses. I lives Lench road. I worked in the Park, reared them long-tailed birds."

"Pheasants, you myuns," Art's uncle replied. "Faizons they calls um over Gloucester Road."

The oak tree nodded more and more as the steam and smoke puffed from Harry Stokes's engine.

"He's beginning to talk, you," Hellfire Jack called from the butt of the tree.

Mr Grove came along and told Hellfire Jack to get four strong labouring men with axes and mattocks to cut the roots of the tree underground.

"I'm afraid Harry will break the cable if he puts too much strain on it," he explained.

As the blades severed the roots the General ordered all his men away from the thick stumpy tree. Taking over for a little time from his foreman he shouted, "Now, Harry, pull steady and I think the tree will fall." *Chuff, chuff, chuff*, the engine puffed more steam, the cable strained and the tree leant towards the engine as the cable was wound up under her boiler. With a crash the tree fell among the thorns. Art wiped his brow, turned to the General and said, "Thur that tree was quicker coming down than growing up, Sir."

As the General walked away, he thought that once more in his life of land clearance and reclamation, his gang were working well and glancing back at the fallen tree saw how even one tree with a big top can cover so much ground.

"Now, my buoys," Art shouted, "let's have the limbs off him." So once more the axes echoed through the waste land as they cut the branches from the fallen tree. Another gang near by under Eli stoked a great fire of wood and bramble, dragging the limbs of oak to be turned to red ashes in the heat of the great fire.

So day after day the work went on. Some days the parts of the jungle-like waste were blackberry bushes and sally elder mixed with hawthorn.

The General's strong army soon cleared patches of this kind.

Then, when the engines were busy, both Harry's and Bill's and Nailus's team hauled more coal, tipping the cartload near the engine's firebox.

Harry and Bill had a code: one blast on the steam whistle of an engine meant stop, two blasts was a signal to pull or release the cable. On the very stubborn trees two cables were hitched to the upper branches so that the tree could be rocked to and fro to loosen the roots.

Hellfire Jack Ellison of Kersoe climbed the trees and fastened the wire ropes. This woodman of great experience had worked for another general, a real army general in a park on Bredon slopes.

Three blasts on the whistle made Nailus swear; it was a call for coal.

"Damn it," he told Harry, "the minute I be gone away to the coal dump you starts blowing that steamer, then when I've sweated my guts out to load a cart and bring my hosses nearly on the trot, you buent out of coal—thurs a damn graet yup lying beside the Black Hoss."

"All right, Nailus," Harry replied with a grin as he stood on the footplate of his engine, the flywheel just turning slowly like a windmill on a calm day. "I don't want to run out of coal, see. This engine is devilish hungry, I won't take long to burn a ton."

Four blasts on the whistle and Albert had to make haste with the water cart. Albert was what Art called 'a gallus young mortal full of oafishness,' he said.

When Albert came with the water he told Old Parker's son, a lad of his own age, that if the Stokes engines blew four blasts too often he would stop their gallup. "How bist going to do that then?" young Parker asked him."

"Oi fill the cart up at that muddy pond by the deer park, and choke the tubes up with mud on the steam engines that's all make um quiet."

Young Parker told his father, who warned Albert not to be so foolish.

In four long years when five hundred men worked Winter and Summer, living as they did in army-like conditions during the week and taking the occasional weekend off to see their families in Wales or the Black Country, there were deaths. The hard graft of the work at Bevington was quite wearing even to those strong men used to long hours.

Rev Cuthbert buried such men in Netherstone churchyard. Some were laid to rest in villages around Lench. Others were buried in their home towns and villages.

Cuthbert did have a problem however during the last year of the stocking of the Waste. It was the wish of a family of a labourer from the Black Country that his body be cremated. Rev Cuthbert quoted in his magazine the Bishop of Lincoln who was against cremation:

Some persons advocate a return to the Pagan practice of Cremation. Christianity has discontinued this from early years. If the bodies of the dead were committed to Public Furnaces for extinction Christianity would suffer no less than public morality and happiness. I mention Cremation to condemn it.

In olden times the dead were wrapped in a shroud, the rich in stone coffins. No-one wants to keep a corpse, the body is dead, and to dust it must return. Laid in favourable earth it is gradually, inoffensively absorbed by the soil in 10 years.

Coffins extend the process. I have seen bodies after 70 years still much the same as when buried and know of one yard where the dead buried in the reign of Charles II are in the same condition. The exhalations from such a mass of boxed up putridity caused the living to suffer in health; that is what we are doing with our strong and costly coffins dishonouring the dead, poisoning the living, abusing the great gifts of a friendly earth of which our bodies are so much a part. The earth to earth coffins which I advocate, made of compressed paper, soon disintegrate. Shakespeare knew what he meant respecting Ophelia.

'Lay her in the earth and from her fair and unpolluted flesh, May violets spring'.

"Strong words in the monthly magazine," Joe Badger told his customers of the Cider Mill.

"Well," Aaron Hicks replied, "it's only the Bishop's words, but the earth is friendly right enough."

Nailus sat with his pint, contemplating. Then he rose from his seat laughing. "Dos't know what tickles me, neighbours, it's like this. The well-to-do as get buried in strong oak be longer going back to dust than the pauper buried by the parish rates in a cheap box. See, the rich be lined in with lead and it's right as the Parson says ashes to ashes dust to dust."

"What's the difference between dust and ashes, you," George Barnes blurted out over the froth of his Saturday beer.

"I'll tell ya what it is, when folks comes out yer from the towns they got different ways and we should repect them," Harry Stokes added.

Nailus sighed knowing that his days at Netherstone were numbered and called Mary Badger, "Draw me another pint a cider and let's be more cheerful. I bin told by Wilf tonight the Black 'Osses be coming away from the Waste until the men to have finished grubbing up the small scrubby bushes. I be gwain thatch the corn ricks, in fact I be gwain to teach young Albert."

Mary smiled and drew him his cider from the barrel. "A teacher now you are, Nailus. That's one up, isn't it?"

"Well," Nailus said, "somebody's got to carry on when I can't mount the ladders any more. Albert's gwain to split the withies for rick pegs, help me to make straw ropes with a scud winder to hold the straw thatch on."

Monday morning Albert and Nailus started thatching a wheat rick ten yards long and seven yards wide.

First they watered the thatching straw, then Nailus showed Albert how to draw the straw in straight bunches with the ears one way into what he called yelms. Three yelms are placed side by side at the eaves of the rick with the ears of straw towards the ridge. Then another such lot of straw is placed above it overlapping it. The first course so laid is as broad at the top as the bottom. Pegs of withy are pushed into the straw forming what is known as the first stektch. When one end of the rick is reached the courses become packed or pointed, being much broader at the eaves than the ridge, until the ridge needs only a handful of straw; this happens half way round the end or width of the rick.

A ten-yard rick takes eight courses or stektches, the straw is held on by the bands twisted around the rick pegs.

Straw band making is quite simple with wet straw, the scud winder being like a primitive brace and bit with a hook on the end, which winds the straw when the brace is turned, until the straw band is long enough to go the full length of the rick.

Bundles of straw are laid across the ridge of the rick to hold the thatch on the top; this is called the Dead Man.

Young Albert with his cord trousers padded at the knees with sacking was soon up and down the ladder waiting on Nailus.

"Pad yer knees, buoy, and save the bruises from the ladder rounds [rungs]," Nailus told him.

And so Albert learnt the art of thatching, but Nailus warned him, "Don't thee get too cock sure; house thatching's a different card, takes years to learn."

Mathison and Samson's idea was to plant the whole of the Waste land with corn, but first it had to be drained.

Teams of horses and carts hauled the pipes from Oathill Station to drain 385 acres of land. Mr Grove's knowledge of the secrets of land drainage was unrivalled; he was a past master at the art.

Ditches were dug to take the water to Bevington Brook and the tile drain pipes were laid in trenches.

Mr Grove owned four brickyards producing bricks as well as drainage pipes.

How well he had planned his operations in co-operation with

railway companies. His special trains were like troop trains which arrived at Oathill Station, with the difference that here were men in corduroy waistcoats sleeved with cotton, heavy boots and gaiters, a cloth-capped brigade instead of a uniformed army.

It's interesting to muse for a while at the character of such men. There would be honest young fellows anxious to break the ties of home and gain extra wages rather than exist on the poor farms of mountainous Wales. Older men shrivelled by the blast furnaces and smelting works of Tipton and Smethwick, happy to breathe once more the pure air of coppice and woodland, to turn from the sledgehammer to the axe and live with living things, the birds the trees and the rabbits. A motley crowd; one would think it was only too likely that friction would exist when the sun went down and the beer flowed. Boots and Booker worked under Eli Anker woodman or forester but not of the same standing as Hellfire Jack of Kersoe.

Jack, with his sharp seven-pound axe swinging all day like a clock pendulum, cut through the oak and hawthorn as if it was butter. Boots and Booker had a bet that they could beat him or better still beat each other.

"Cut that ash plant through, Booker, and then I'll cut the one anant."

Boots boasted, "I'll cut it in four draws with my axe."

Hellfire Jack stood and watched these hobbledehoys as he called the youths, drive the steel into the green wood.

Boots managed his in four blows and Booker took five. It was agreed that the loser paid for a quart of ale at the Wheelbarrow and Castle at Radford. As the sun fell over Bredon Slopes that night and the thirsty men quaffed their beer from the barrel, Hellfire Jack reminded Booker he had a score to pay to Boots.

"I a paid for a quart a while ago," the Black Country lad answered.

"Indeed you have not, mun," came the reply from Boots of the Black Mountains, and in a few seconds each youth stripped to the waist took up position in the one end of the long bar, as the fists were flying and Hellfire Jack stood near to see that the bare knuckles were aimed at the targets allowed. The bets were laid on Boots or Booker.

Round after round the swollen-eyed lads threw their punches and the blood ran freely from hammered noses.

Nailus and George sat and watched the young men fight as they had never seen fighting before.

"I lay tanner on the Welsh buoy," Nailus placed his money on the upturned barrel.

"And I'll lay a tanner on the Black Country lad," George replied.

Eli Ankers held the money. The youths stopped as the land-lady came and wiped their bloody faces with a flannel.

"Have another pint a piece," Hellfire Jack offered and the mugs frothed with good measure, Malvern measure, the land-lord said.

The fight went on until both men shook hands. They had had enough so Eli gave the stake money back to the men from the Waste who had hoped to win a drink or two.

In the morning as the General rode round on his cob he saw the swollen eyes and bruised noses of the two young men.

"Foolish to fight you know, when the liquor gets you argu-mentative. Besides the job here at Bevington is almost complete, Harry Stokes and his brother Bill will then plough the Waste with the steam tackle."

Mr Mathison and Tom Samson arrived and were pleased with the position in which the clay drain pipes were laid, every drain having a slight fall to a larger master drain to empty into the brook. Before the soil was shovelled into the drain trenches to cover the pipes, Mr Grove instructed Hellfire Jack to teach some of the men to make faggots or bundles of ash wood and bind them with withy. These faggots placed on top of the pipes allowed the water to percolate through the soil and drain away. So the Waste was cleared.

Mr Grove then saw the landlord of the Wheelbarrow and Castle and arranged a feast for some of the workers who had worked four long years at clearing the Waste. As the ale flowed as never before a song was sung by the men. A song composed by Arthur Allchurch of South Littleton, near Evesham, to the tune 'Auld Lang Syne'.

Come all you jolly labouring
   men and listen to my song.
The theme is well known to you all; it is of Bevington.
Five years ago, great oaks did grow mid thorns and briars long.
But now the labouring men have made cornfields of Bevington.

Chorus: For George and Dick and Fred, Old Parker and his son
And Art and John and Alf and Tom, they all worked at
   Bevington.

Some folk did say, and well they may, it never would be done.
But when did brave hearts ever fall when backed by arms so
   strong?
So cheerily we went to work with spades and mattocks long.
Though many weary bones we brought from the work at
   Bevington.

When nearly done, then like a man up Mr Webb did come.
Said he, "I will stand treat, my men, when ere this job is
   done."
He left a pound to buy some drink, and didn't we have fun;
And Boots and Booker had a fight at the Wake of Bevington.

And now the job is done and o'er my song I now will end.
Heaven bless the fruits of this our toil and on us blessings send;
In years to come, passing this way, our earthly course near run,
We'll proudly say we mind the day we grubbed up Bevington.

So Boots and Booker did have another encounter at the Wake. The song was sung for years after in the Wheelbarrow and Castle to keep alive the memory of strong men, stout hearts and the skill of Mr Grove, the enterprise of Mr Mathison and Tom Samson.

Nailus planted the first crop of wheat with two horses on a five-furrow drill. Wilf Cob put the Stokes brothers to work planting and harrowing.

The boys of ten years of age of Netherstone rode over on the carts those frosty October mornings to lead the horses over virgin land and as the lunch-time fire burned low Nailus said:

"I suppose we be like prospectors like they be in America."

And so ended a marathon task of reclamation where following the corn crops, orchards of apples and plums made pink and white rows of petal scent in the one time waste land.

Rev Cuthbert held a service of thanksgiving to God for giving strength to men of muscle who cleared Bevington Waste.

"My theme to-day, friends," he preached to a packed church, "is not a usual topic. It is not 'Remember Lot's Wife', it's 'Remember Bevington Waste', an achievement by our neighbours supported by help from all parts of this Island."

16

At Pershore, Where D'Ye Think?

As Wilf Cob had proved himself to be such a successful Bailiff under Mathison and Samson, they promoted him still higher and made him responsible for the whole of the estate. Young Edward Mathison had finished at school and he took charge of the Home Farm as Samson's Farm was called.

Wilf had been successful in seeing Mr Grove's scheme through in the stocking of Bevington Waste and he became increasingly interested in fruit farming.

A man named Crooke had discovered a useful plum tree growing among the trees in Tydesley Wood. It seemed that this tree had fallen from the stars. The fruit was golden yellow.

"The colour of a sovereign," Nailus said, "I an't sin many sovereigns, but the old chap did have a spade guinea."

Mr Crooke dug up the tree and there had been speculation in the Cider Mill years before as to how it would develop.

"Grows from a sucker," George Barnes declared. "No need to bud or graft him."

Among the trees at the Grange Wilf had planted three of these Pershore plums. He and Gwen had kept every sucker which grew from its roots. Stocked sway from the parent tree, they grew in the black soil of the Grange into useful trees.

"Have you enough Pershore plum trees to plant a part of Bevington Waste?" Monty Mathison suddenly became interested in a scheme to grow plums.

The trees at the Grange bore what Nailus described as a clinking crop of fruit; he and George Barnes picked the lower branches with twenty-rung ladders. Aaron, a man of the trees who practised some forestry as well as the preservation of game, was a handy man with a ladder, a man who with a pick basket slung on his back by a broad leather waist belt, climbed to the tops and gathered some of the best of the plums. Albert with horse and spring cart hauled the fruit to Oathill Station, loading it in trucks for cities of the North. Carrying the plums in pot hampers made from the osiers of the River Avon each holding 72 lb, Albert worked backwards and forward in time to catch the afternoon goods train.

As Squire Mathison and Tom Samson visited the orchard one August afternoon, pleased with the produce of the trees and Wilf's foresight, Nailus cleared his throat from fifteen rungs up his short ladder and spoke these words:

"Master Mathison and Master Samson, you be the men as pays on Saturdays."

The Squire and his partner looked up into the tree where Nailus foraged with his horny hands among the leaves for the golden fruit.

"Well, what of it, Nailus?" Monty Mathison replied. "Aren't you satisfied with your half sovereign a week, and a cottage?"

"Oh yes I be satisfied, but George and I have been thinking about the fruit on the ground among the grass being devoured by the wops [wasps]. 'Tis shameful, Sir."

"What do you suggest, Nailus? We can't put inferior fruit in the hampers and send that by rail to Manchester and Liverpool."

Nailus came down the ladder with his peck basket full of golden plums. "Lovely sample, eh, Tom?" Monty commented. Tom nodded and looked at Nailus and George wondering what was on their minds.

"Can we pick these plums up after tea, Sir?" Nailus turned to the Squire "and put them in a borrel [barrel]."

The employers of the Netherstone Farm laughed when they realised what Nailus's idea was.

"Of course," Monty replied. "And no doubt you have got your eyes on a fresh empty wine cask from Joe Badger."

"Well, he has got a sixty-gallon one that we can have," George Barnes spoke from the top of his ladder.

"Plum wine, eh?" Monty replied.

"Well, Sir, we allus calls it Plum Jerkum in the village, and very nice it is when it's made right. Yunt that right, Aaron?"

Aaron was just topping the next tree with his longer ladder. "Oh yes," the keeper said, "but it's potent and I would warn your carter and shepherd that it's not to be drunk in quarts like cider."

After tea the old men got Albert, Ruth, Jane and Kate to bring the clothes basket and pick up the fallen fruit into it.

"Damn my rags," Nailus told George, "we shall want more than one sixty-gallon barrel from the Cider Mill."

The fallen plums were soon fermenting in the cask. The wasps followed but the golden juice left the plum stones and skins and wine was made at Netherstone.

The name of Sep Sands had never been forgotten in the village. The Major and Rosemary had now two daughters living in their home on the Downs. Lewes had died, so Sep was in charge of the Major's stable. As Albert Barnes took yet another load of plums to Oathill Station Sep arrived off the afternoon train.

"Who do you work for, young fella," were Sep's first words to young Albert.

"Master Mathison and Master Samson. You wouldn't know them they be good gaffers and my eyes, ant we had a tally ho crop of plums."

Sep looked at the horse in the shafts of the cart loaded with hampers. He ran his professional hands down its legs, picked each hoof up by the fetlock and remarked, "Useful animal. Has the gelding been backed?" Before Albert could reply, Sep opened the horse's mouth, looked at its teeth and pronounced "Two years old."

"You know a bit about hosses, Sir?" Albert said. " 'Cos 'Persha Plum' is two years old. Last May just as the plum blossom set and the trees were in leaf he was dropped by a half-legged mare in the orchard, and he has been backed only by me when I ride him from the field to the stable. Promise me, Sir, you won't tell our Dad, but I jump every field gate early mornings when I get him into the yard, that's with only a halter on. Aaron Hicks knows and says he a natural jumper.''

"Aaron Hicks? I knew him and Nailus when I worked here at the Grange.'' There was a touch of a deep longing for the past in Sep's voice as he spoke to Albert.

That night Sep stayed at Widow Prew's cottage but next morning he made himself known to Tom Samson.

"Come on in, boy,'' Sarah Samson said. "How's the Major and Rosemary?''

"Oh fine, Mrs Samson, but poor Lewes has passed over. Yes, the old warrior has left his riding boots hung among the harness and a photo which the Major has hung in our stable.''

"What's your business, Sep?'' Tom asked bluntly, remembering that years ago Sep had caused trouble on the estate.

"I've come here,'' Sep said, "to have a look around the old haunts on my way to Wales to buy useful looking hurdlers for the Major to race. And I think you have one.''

"My one hunter is not on the market and I am sure the Squire has nothing to offer.''

"That's as maybe,'' Sep replied, "but I've met Albert taking plums to the station with a horse which should be on the racecourse. I'll buy him, Mr Samson, and pay you a good price.''

"See me this evening, Sep, after there has been chance to have a word with Mr Mathison and Wilf.''

"Wilf?'' Sep exclaimed. "What position does he hold here, then?''

"Oh, just Bailiff, head Bailiff over six thousand acres of land. Good day to you, Sep.''

That day the Squire, Tom and Wilf, knowing that the plum season was nearly over thought carefully about selling 'Persha Plum'.

"Ask him a hundred guineas," was Wilf's suggestion. The Partners agreed that there were other horses which Albert could use to drive to town to fetch the seed corn from the station or take a few lambs or a calf to market.

Sep arrived at the Grange that evening and bought 'Persha Plum', railing him at Oathill Station the day following.

At the Cider Mill while George and Nailus supped their pints Albert came in and in Nailus's words was 'crying like a babby'.

"What's wrong?" George muttered as he met him, ducking under the low beams of the inglenook to meet Albert.

"They have sold my hoss to Sep for a man named Major Forbrooke or summat," Albert sobbed out. " My 'Persha Plum'."

Old Nailus turned to Mary Badger and wiping the cider from his whiskers, sat with tears in his eyes, and felt the pangs in his heart that he had experienced when so often Tom Samson had sold a useful horse in the team in the last few years.

"Bless ya, Mary," he said. "I was mortal glad to get rid of Captain and Colonel in a manner of speaking, they didn't turn enough furrows over in a day to satisfy me, let alone the Gaffer. 'Tis different when you have got a young gain animal."

"Unt that the same with a sheep dog, George," he asked his drinking partner.

So much was happening at Oathill, it is sufficient to say that 'Persha Plum' won a hurdle race for the Major the following March at Cheltenham. Sep had proved a shrewd buyer. Even the Rev Cuthbert was pleased that a foal dropped in the Grange orchard had proved a winner. Quoting from his Bible to Aunt Hannah he said, "Aunt, don't think that this is a good simile, but we read that the stone which the builders rejected has become the chief cornerstone, how one underestimates animals, horses, dogs, and how one underestimates people. Who would have thought a few years ago that Wilf would be responsible for the husbandry of so many acres of land?"

"Gwen has been a stay to him, Bob," the old lady replied.

"A pity that you had not married and not been dependent on an old spinster like me to keep house for you."

"Oh, please forget it, Aunt! I once loved Gwen, but it was not to be. She chose Wilf and Gwen chose well, but I loved her dearly from the moment she came here from Brecon."

" 'Persha Plum'. What an apt name for a horse from this land where the blow, as Shakespeare calls the blossom on the trees, lies across these little hills and vales like sparkling snow in the springtime."

Hannah sighed as she poked the dying embers of the late night fire and added, "Yes, 'tis how I imagine the Garden of Eden was before men spoilt it; then it became like Bevington Waste, briars and thistles. God made the country beautiful, Bob, but men have to keep it so."

The Marquis, encouraged by what he had seen in the improvement of his land by Mathison and Samson and how Wilf had grown such fruit, was not satisfied by the Golden Pershore Plums but had now planted some acres of Martin's Seedlings, a purple plum which Walter Martin had introduced into the area by pollinating the Old Blue Diamond with the Early Prolific.

More tenants of the Marquis planted plums on the land between Lench and Bredon but Pershore, which from time immemorial had been famous for its perry made from the juice of the pears growing along the riverside, became the Capital of Plum Growing.

The year we have been covering was a good year for plums. The smaller growers had those little extras which make life more tolerable. They sang a new song in the little town.

PERSHORE

But as to Pershore and her plums
Her riches are untold
When all her trees are bearing down
Beneath their weight of Gold.
Oh then her lads and lasses there

Are all a merry crew
I trow they jest from morn to night
And pipe and carol too
But such a song as they might sing
Here let me sing to you.

PERSHORE, WHERE D'YE THINK?

You ask me where and whence I come,
   From Pershore, where d'ye think?
Where do we grow the yellow plum?
   Why, Pershore, where d'ye think?
Hop gatherers jest in ribald vein
   O'er clustering hops they pull;
While farmers reap the golden grain,
   And pack their granaries full,
But we, content in merriment,
   Will let the glasses clink,
For all is peace and plenty,
   At Pershore, where d'ye think?—
   At Pershore, where d'ye think?
   At Pershore, where d'ye think?
For all is peace and plenty,
   At Pershore, where d'ye think?

Where do the trees hang down with gold?
   At Pershore, where d'ye think?
And where produce a hundredfold?
   Why, Pershore, where d'ye think?
Klondyke can yield her yellow vein,
   And vaunt her glittering ore;
And we who chaunt the glad refrain
   Can boast of fruitful store;
And Jill is blest, and Jack is blest,
   And Jack and Jill can link,
For all is peace and plenty,

At Pershore, where d'ye think?—
At Pershore, where d'ye think?
At Pershore, where d'ye think?
For all is peace and plenty.
At Pershore, where d'ye think?

Where do the churchbells peal in tune?
At Pershore, where d'ye think?
Where brightest shines the harvest moon?
Why, Pershore, where d'ye think?
For Pershore brightly smiles the morn,
And fairly sets the sun;
There Ceres bears the brimful horn,
And all is mirth and fun,
Let who will come to harvest home
In joy to feast and drink,
For all is peace and plenty,
At Pershore, where d'ye think?
At Pershore, where d'ye think?
At Pershore, where d'ye think?
For all is peace and plenty,
At Pershore, where d'ye think?

O, Heav'n hath blest us from His store,
At Pershore, where d'ye think?
And whom will Heaven bless the more?
Why Pershore, whom d'ye think?
While Nature smiles her blandest smile,
And heaps the festive board,
Arise, ye hardy sons of toil,
Arise and thank the Lord.
For Pershore's sake that ne'er the cake,
Nor cruse of oil may sink,
But all is peace and plenty,
At Pershore, where d'ye think?

At Pershore, where d'ye think?
At Pershore, where d'ye think?
But all is peace and plenty,
At Pershore, where d'ye think?

From 'In the Valley of the Gods', by W. D. Vizard, F.R.H.S.

17

The Sunday Dig

ALL AROUND PERSHORE THE LITTLE MEN HAD PLANTED the yellow egg plum in plantations of four to eight acres. Every part of Netherstone which was sheltered from the north-east winds, awkward shaped stretches of land known as 'gores' grew plums.

The Marquis let out at reasonable rents such small holdings to the little master men, men from Evesham with market gardening experience.

"We ull damn soon be like the Garden of Eden," Nailus's loosened tongue echoed in Joe Badger's kitchen.

"That was a apple as Eve tempted Adam with, you old fool," George Barnes was riled with Nailus, partly because he had planted egg plums in his garden to make a few shillings extra in the summer time.

"I beunt a Bible thumper, but Cuthbert allus said it was the serpent as caused the trouble," Nailus replied with a twinkle in his eye, at the same time putting his crock mug on the table in front of Mary Badger.

"Another pint?" Mary questioned.

"Oi, another drop of apple juice. It seems as if we must keep in the garden of Eden tonight."

Harry and Bill Stokes sat there without a smile on their faces looking towards Nailus and the fire.

"What's up, neighbours?" George asked.

"Is something worrying you both?"

"Thee tell um, Harry," said Bill nudging him almost hard enough to spill his cider.

Bill's eyes were watery, partly because of the stinging smoke from the Cider Mill chimney, but mainly because of their trouble. He then opened up his story to one and all under Joe Badger's roof.

"'Tis like this," he said. "Our nephew came down to a little village under Bredon a feow years ago and took some land off the Marquis about six acres. He's done well so far, sending gillies [wallflowers] to Evesham market and strawberries, his plum trees unt hardly established enough to bear much fruit, but they be growing." Bill supped again at his cider. "Alf Rogers our nephew this Winter has all of a sudden bin crippled with harthritis in both of his hips and can just about momble about the house."

A hush fell over the Mill pub until young Albert asked, "What about his ground? Is it dug for his early peas or his sprouts? If it isn't it will need doing soon, so that the frost will lax the clay ready for the planting."

Harry wiped a tear from his eye with the spotted handkerchief he took from under his belt and said, "It's the same as it was before Christmas. Young Alf hasn't been able to do a stroke of work all the Winter and he's a missus and five kids to feed."

As the Netherstone men went up the wooden hill to bed that night one thought filled their minds—Alf Rogers' undug land and Alf Rogers' wife and children.

Next morning Nailus spoke to Wilf in the stable about Alf's predicament.

"I'd plough his ground with your permission, but it unt so easy, it's partly planted with young trees and it's got to be dug."

Wilf nodded, inquiring of Nailus whereabouts around the Hill Alf's land lay.

"Is it a part of Calves Gore?" the young Bailiff asked. "That part the Marquis has let to the tenants for fruit and vegetable growing."

"You be right, 'tis sticky ground, needs turning over smartish quick to catch the Spring frosts."

Meanwhile Joe Badger had an idea. He met the villagers in the Cider Mill and suggested that the only way to keep Alf afloat was to dig his ground.

"But we be at work all the wick," Harry Stokes replied. "It only leaves Sunday."

"The better the day the better the deed," George Barnes replied, "I'd help to dig on Sunday." To a man, every one of Joe's customers agreed to walk to Calves Gore on the Sunday and dig enough land for Alf to plant in the Spring. Other able bodied men who heard of the scheme were eager to join in.

What a sight it was that following Sunday, a typical February day! The early morning frost had knitted the top two inches of clay just enough to prevent it lovingly clinging to the men's boots.

It was left to Harry Stokes to tell the men which part of the smallholding to dig.

Twenty-five men with forks stood on the head-land; men who were aged like Nailus down to boys who hadn't long left school.

"Reminds me of Bevington Waste, so to speak," Nailus said as he put his hob-nailed boots on his fork and turned over the first spit of land.

The men worked in rows of five, keeping a straight trench like a furrow as they turned over the sods.

"Funny how the birds comes and feeds on the worms, Sunday dinner, I suppose," George Barnes remarked to his partner facing the trench, Nailus, of course.

"Oi, and yer comes our dinner," Nailus replied. The men straightened their backs, took their jackets from the hedge where the hoar frost had thawed to silvery drops of water in the weak midday sun of February.

Along the head-land came Kate, Jane, Gwen, Ruth and Mary, the wives or mothers of the Sunday diggers, with cloth-covered plates of Sunday dinner.

As they sat in line under the head-land hedge and ate the steaming potatoes, greens and meat, Joe Badger arrived with enough cider to quench their thirsts.

Joe had come over in his horse and trap bringing with him the women who lived at Netherstone and between there and Calves Gore and their men's dinner.

"Come on, my boys," Aaron Hicks spoke up. "It will be dark at five o'clock, let's get this little job done before then."

The men were soon back with their forks, some digging between Alf's strawberry rows, some between his asparagus while others dug the open land between the rows of young fruit trees where Alf's early peas would be planted and his sprouts.

Occasionally the forks turned up a potato left in the ground from last year. Nailus put these in a pick basket to take to Alf.

"They ull be glad of ever tater. Five youngsters takes some fittle, yunt that right, Aaron?" he added.

Aaron stood straight in his keepers' breeches and speaking quietly to Nailus, told him that Tom Samson had asked him to leave a rabbit at Alf's house every weekend.

"That's what I calls Christian." And no sooner had Nailus said the word than Rev Cuthbert arrived.

"Good afternoon, men, and God bless you," the Vicar said in a louder voice than usual so that all twenty-five of the diggers could hear.

"Be us a doing right then, Vicar, a breaking the Sabbath for once?" the old carter asked.

"Indeed you are doing right, neither are you breaking the Sabbath. Does not it say in the Book, that 'if an ox or an ass fall into a pit on the Sabbath will ye not pull him out'. Alf Rogers is in a deep pit at the moment; I've called on him he is delighted at your kind action. This is the good Samaritan all over again; I am proud of my parishioners. Lend me your fork, Nailus, and let me dig a few sods," and taking Nailus's fork Rev Cuthbert felt that he was showing that he meant what he said.

Alf's land was dug that Sunday. As the frosts laxed the turned earth producing a tilth fit for planting, Alf got stronger and was able to start work on his holding.

So Alf Rogers was saved from going on the Parish with his

family or living meagrely off the rates. His independence was nearly lost when his health failed, but the kind neighbours of his native Vale rescued him like a brand from the burning.

Rev Cuthbert left no doubt in the minds of the Parish that the Sunday dig was an exceptional action of neighbourliness on the part of the workers.

'Mark you,' he wrote in his magazine, 'I would not countenance this sort of thing if it happened without there being a serious emergency.'

However there were two young men who rented a holding off the Marquis; two men who lived on the extreme edge of Netherstone where Mathison and Samson's land met up with the Marquis's.

These men arrived some weeks after the dig and had little regard for the Church. After morning prayer as beginners in the art of cultivating soil they spent their Sundays looking around the village holdings studying how the locals grew their crops.

Bob Cuthbert hit hard at this practice in his magazine. Under a heading 'Sunday Observance' he wrote:

The Lord's Day as the first day of the week has always been called has been given us by The Lord. First that it might be a day exclusively devoted to worship, acts of devotion and meditation on God's word, and Second, a day of rest from worldly labour in order that it may be devoted to spiritual work.

We have great regret in observing that lately as the summer months are here some of our people neglect the evening service, and may be seen going for walks as the Bells ring for Evensong.

For this there is no excuse whatever. Our people are not town people shut up in stuffy shops or in close and noisy factories all the week living in back slums, where nothing beautiful ever meets the eye, but we are in the open gardens and fields from Monday until Saturday getting quite as much bodily exercise as we require. A walk on Sunday evening? Surely the afternoon will suffice?

What a spectacle for angels to behold the followers of Christ turning their back on the Church door, when the bells ring.

What would the heathen think of such a spectacle? He hears the white man sneer at idolatry but what does the white man do?

Surely it's better to worship something than nothing. The heathen who goes to his idol's temple and worships the best he knows wouldn't dream of neglecting this just for the whim of taking a walk. This is an act of irreverence terrible closely akin to an insult to Almighty God.

Gladstone attends church three times a day and calls people who attend once 'oncers'.

So the Sunday Dig did two things for Netherstone and district: it proved that the brotherhood of man was there at the time it was needed. It gave Bob Cuthbert a chance to explain to his flock the difference between extreme crisis and what he thought to be neglect in worship in his Parish.

"Plain speaking," Nailus said to George Barnes. "'Tis like yer. I udn't put it past them two fellas as no doubt he is hitting at stealing a bit of early gilly flower seed when we are all in church. It ha' been done and a sprout stem pulled up laden with seed ready to thresh has been known to be stolen from our holding and locked away in a hovel."

"You see, George," Nailus explained it, "you be a Market Gardener and can get your produce on the market just a week before the usual time, that's were the money's made and the men on the holdings prides themselves on seeding their own strain of cabbage, sprouts, gillies and keeping it for themselves."

18

In Like a Lion, Out Like a Lamb

'IN LIKE A LION, OUT LIKE A LAMB'. THESE WORDS uttered by Nailus every Spring referred of course to the month of March. Another of his favourite sayings was 'Never come March, never come Winter'.

Hellfire Jack from Kersoe, who had made a little money helping to clear Bevington Waste, had taken one of the Marquis's holdings to rent at what was known as the Goldfields; probably so named because of its wealth of Golden Pershore egg plums.

Boots and Booker were his neighbours and life-long friends. They shared a hovel together, a brick-built shed with a fireplace and copper furnace boiler. Here they ate their twelve o'clock dinner.

Every Vale gardener was used to dining at twelve.

In the copper boiler they brewed the wine, home-made, potent it was. They also used to boil the pig potatoes, 'chats' as they were called.

Hellfire Jack, despite his name, had been with Boots and Booker helping to dig Alf Rogers' land on that memorable Sunday. March came in like a lion and as Hellfire Jack and his neighbours went home from the Cider Mill in early March walking together up the slopes of Netherstone Hill, the moon stood in the sky over the coppice like a golden waggon wheel. The stars were keen. Boots looked to the north and pointed out the Plough or Jack-and-his-waggon, as the locals preferred to call that group of twinkling silver pieces near the Pole Star.

"Smells like a frost." Jack spoke next as he sniffed the cold clear air.

As the men followed the cart track to their cottages, walking on the green sward between the wheel ruts, a sea of mist lay still and quiet over the Goldfields.

"That's where it ull be rimy or hoary in the morning," Booker pointed out. He knew that the mists on the low land where the brook made for the river was a certain sign of March frosts.

"Me and the missus picked all our gilly flowers that were in bud this afternoon," Jack remarked. "They be stood up in baths of water in our kitchen bunched with raffia. No doubt the heat of the fire will bring them into flower in a day or two." Jack laughed to himself, then said, "There won't be no glut of gillies in the market after tonight, it's going to be a sharpest frost you ever knew, you chaps."

"Well, the plum blow [blossom] unt out and the hedges are bare, naked as Winter apart from the blackthorn bushes and the elder."

As the men walked near the hedge in the light of the moon the hawthorn was not in bud, but the blossom of the blackthorn or sloes showed snow white on the Hill.

"The blackthorn Winter," Boots remarked.

The morning frost was sharp turning the dewdrops on the Goldfields hedges to snowy white.

"A white world," Jack greeted his neighbours with as they lit the wood fire in the hovel.

A few days later Jack's gillies had flowered in the shallow baths of water in front of his grate.

"What a sight, a carpet of red velvet ready for packing in pot hampers for market!"

Then Jack drove his pony and spring cart to market to get the top price with his flowers.

Old Nailus warned Jack to be careful with his market money as the frost had knocked the rows of gilly flowers back in the Goldfield plantation and it would be weeks before they would bloom again.

"Dost know what our old chap used to say, Nailus?" Jack answered. "Thurs no taste nor smell to nothing. He was right, you know that gilly money ull tide us over, happen."

Up on the hill George Barnes' ewes were lambing, in fact they had almost finished. George told his wife Ruth that there was one half bred Suffolk very deceiving.

"Ewes be deceiving," he said. "Sometimes they be big bellied through eating a gutsfull of roots. I've known un lamb after the May shearing, but I'll risk that ewe and put her with the barren sheep."

That night Ruth woke to hear the bleating of the barren ewes. George slipped on his trousers over his night shirt, put on his top coat and in sockless boots made for the commotion.

Ruth followed and once again the March moon shone bright enough to read the headlines of a newspaper.

"Stand behind the bushes, Ruth, while I get closer to the ewe." And there before his eyes he saw plainly that Suffolk ewe with one lamb at her feet which she licked and was loath to leave. As the pains came once more she stretched on the turf with her nostrils open and her belly straining to give birth to another lamb.

A fox grovelled on the moonlit turf like a trained sheep dog, edging nearer, trying to steal the new-born lamb while the ewe was giving birth to her second.

The ewe got up once more between pains. She stamped her feet, butted towards the thief who retreated towards the coppice, then she returned to her lamb and like a shot George gripped her as she lay once more on the turf and helped her to drop her second lamb.

The fox now gave up and returned to the coppice as George shouted and Ruth walked towards the barn, the ewe followed and there on a bed of straw he left the mother and her two youngsters safely for the night.

"The hounds meet at the Cider Mill tomorrow," George whispered as he made the stairs creak under his bare feet, "and I hope they will give Master Reynard a good run to the other side of the hill.''

Nailus, although he still worked for Mathison and Samson, took great interest in 'the Little Men' as he called the market gardeners at the Goldfields and Calves Gore.

Here Hellfire Jack, Boots and Booker worked and Alf Rogers, Harry and Bill Stokes' nephew had his holdings. As April came in with warm Spring weather the villagers knew how fickle that month could be.

''Oi, March don't finish until 12th of April,'' Nailus reminded them, March weather he meant of course.

Clothed in white the plum trees at the Goldfields and indeed the whole Vale was by Easter a mass of bloom. Visitors came by train from Birmingham to see the Vale dressed in her Sunday best.

Some orchards were carpeted by the blood red gilly flowers, others by daffodils.

Rev Cuthbert preached his Easter sermon at Netherstone, reminding his flock that the warm earth gives life to the bitter sloe and the sweet greengage. The cool melon, the fiery mustard, nourishing wheat and deadly nightshade.

How well Bob Cuthbert knew that the well-being of his parish and those around hung in the balance this month, the month of blossom.

On Easter Sunday afternoon old Nailus and George Barnes walked with Jack, Boots, Booker, and Alf through the avenues of blossom, 'blow' as they called it. Wild bees worked tirelessly among that sweet-scented blossom, pollinating as they moved from twig to twig.

''How still it is on a Sunday,'' George remarked as the men leant against a paddock gate where Hellfire Jack's pony was enjoying a good roll in the afternoon sun.

''Oi, the bees be just as busy Sunday as weekday. Just listen to their hum on Jack's 'Prolific' plums and Alf's damsons. Oi, 'tis a strange thing,'' Nailus continued, ''that the early and late plum trees bloom at the same time while the Pershores and Victorias, both main crop, show white a few days later.''

Leaving the plantation the Netherstone men remarked on the lushness of the grass on the roadside verge compared with the close cropped turf on the hill.

George and Nailus went home but the young men climbed Netherstone Hill. Here the lambs thrived on the greening turf, the young rabbits grew, nest and nest emerged from the holts.

The smell of flowers in the Hill Lane, the voice of singing from the woodland birds made Netherstone a good place to live that Easter Sunday afternoon.

''If you can put your foot on nine daisies at a time, our Dad allus reconed Spring had come,'' Jack told his neighbours as they all watched a skylark winging its way up into the blue.

So the young men went home to their Sunday tea enriched by the weekly cake.

Next evening down on the village green the free open green of an English village where a large solitary elm stood towering right in the centre, spreading branches above a rough bench under its trunk, Nailus, George and Aaron sat and talked. How often good tidings and bad tidings had been shared there as the small pale green leaves from its bough showed the sap rising in the Spring of the year.

This is so perfect an English picture to see old men when their day's work is done gather with their smoking pipes of clay. They talk of crops and weather, the health and illnesses of their neighbours, the prosperity or adversity of the village. The children gambol and leapfrog on the common grass, and play with the shepherd's dog.

Old boys listen to the wisdom of the ancients, look for birds' nests, while the girls pick bunches of wild flowers.

Around the green stand the neatly thatched, whitewashed cottages with leaded dormers, large gardens, beehives. As the sun sets on such a scene blue smoke rises in pillars, the church tower in the background, all is silent once more except perhaps just the clap of an old gate, the whistle of a home-going plough-boy, the hooting of the tawny owl.

Here before long every cottage porch will be heavy with the scent of honeysuckle as the year rolls on in Netherstone.

"What of the blow?" The old men on their bench seats have had grave doubts about the plum crop. In fact this has been the evening topic.

"'Tis too early," said one.

"If only we don't get a frost until the leaves open to protect it," said another.

Nightly at the Cider Mill men emptied the crock tots of cider. The chimney from the tap room fire adds its blue smoke to the evening at Netherstone.

But the plum leaves had not opened despite the spells of weak sunshine, only the elder in the hedgebottoms showed much leaf. The bread-and-cheese buds on the hawthorn were swelling to bursting point.

Coo Coo was heard from the coppice, but this was not the note of the cuckoo, he was not due here until about the 19th April, it was the *Coo Coo Coo Coo, My toe bleeds Betty*; the quice or wood pigeon's call. Rooks circled over their nests while the ball-chins or bald chicks lay among the twigs in the greening elms.

When the elm leaves were as big as a farthing it was time to plant runner beans in the garden, and when the elm leaves were as big as a penny you will have to plant if you are going to have any.

Just advice from Nailus to what he called 'the buoy chaps of the Goldfields'.

As the white blossom of the plum trees faded to a creamy brown, the wind blew the petals in showers from the trees.

By careful observation the minute plums could be seen, about the size of a mustard seed. Then came a hot day, so hot that men worked stripped to their braces, dogs panted with dripping tongues, George's lambs stretched sleeping on the warm turf of the hill.

"A weather breeder," Nailus called it as the sun sank behind Netherstone Hill like a ball of fire. As darkness fell the stars shone bright and clear. The trains sounded near on the distant. main line.

"We be in for a reamer tonight," Harry Stokes said as he stood in the doorway of the Cider Mill. Standing there as he often did with his two thumbs under his broad leather belt which surrounded forty-two-inch of belly.

"What makes ya so sure we be gwain to have a frost?" Hellfire Jack questioned him.

"It's no damn good a we staring up at the starry sky. It's cold out yer. Come on into the bar and we'll talk around the fire." As Jack called for drinks for the company, he sat next to the burning logs.

Nailus then began to put his thoughts into words.

"Now, instinct unt confined to animals. They knows when dangers near, but so does I. You all sin the sun go as red as blood to bed tonight, you have sin the stars, yerd the train plain. Have you smelt a frost? 'Cos I have, it comes with experience. The mist has crept up from the river meddas and settled on the Goldfields. That means the frost ull catch the blow on the low-lying field for certain.

"Hasn't ever noticed how weather-wise parsons be? I see Master Cuthbert has lit a fire of couch and other rubbish in his garden among his feow fruit trees. The smoke from that fire ull save his plums, but as for you chaps at the Goldfields, you be in the hands of the Almighty, so to speak."

As the men left the Mill, the chill mist from the Avon river lay knee deep on the fields like the down from a duck's breast. The hoary rime was twinkling in the light of their lanterns as they walked near the roadside verges.

"Only a ground frost yet," Harry said, "but what ull the morning bring?"

George Barnes rose at six next morning and when the first light appeared he saw from his hillside when he had fed the ewes and lambs the Vale below white with frost. The Spring frost had reached from the river to the gate at the bottom of the hillside field. The Goldfields, he thought, 'what's it like down there?' Walking down the hill to see for himself he found the small-holders standing speechless at first by their hovel doors.

Hellfire Jack said, "It has swept the deck, killed all the blow. There won't be enough plums on all these acres to make a plum pudding."

"It's killed the hovels," Booker exclaimed in desperation, "and we shall go hungry to closet."

Then as the sun rose higher over the Cotswolds the scene looked even worse. It was a winter frost which had scythed off the roadside nettles, blackened the eye of every early strawberry blossom.

The plum trees were turned a coffee colour. Ice, twice as thick as a penny, covered the hovel water butts.

The gillies drooped once more, but worst of all the men of the Goldfields had lost their plum crop. Blossom which had delighted the town folk was killed.

Men who had dug and pruned all the winter would this season see nothing but leaves on their trees.

19

The Harvest

MATHISON AND SAMSON NOW REAPED AS FINE A harvest of wheat on Bevington Waste as had ever been seen in the West Midlands.

The stooks stood in rows like the aisles of a cathedral, golden heavy in the ear.

The hot summer had suited the crops here on virgin soil. It's true some of the old arable had not produced such a bumper crop of corn as the sun parched the ground.

But Bevington was full of ploughed-in humus, the leaves of ages acted as a tonic to the roots of wheat. Roots which penetrated deep into the soil to find the moisture.

So Wilf tied his horse to the farm gate and, as he slipped from the saddle hanging his jacket to the bough of a tree, he rolled up his sleeves, took a shuppick or pitchfork and worked with Harry, Bill, George and Nailus, loading the waggons with sheaves. Other gangs worked with the same will at Netherstone Farm.

Joe Badger left his pub to Mary, worked with Albert and Aaron.

The whole countryside echoed with men's voices.

"Hold tight," called the ploughboys.

"Keep that corner in a bit," old Nailus told Harry when Harry built the loads.

The women were singing in the stubble as they stooked the corn still lying where the reapers left the sheaves.

Boots, Booker and Hellfire Jack called at Tom Samson's one August evening and asked for a harvest job on the land.

"Our plum trees be bare in the Goldfields and we be must obliged of the chance to work."

"See Wilf," Tom told them, "and tell Wilf that if he can use you to start you tomorrow."

So the creak of heavy waggons with two horses was constant up Netherstone and Bevington village street.

Boots, Booker, Hellfire Jack and Alf Rogers worked in the rickyard at Bevington unloading the waggons and building the ricks under Nailus's supervision.

Nailus was particular about building 'the Staddle', the foundation of each rick. These staddles of timber which stretched from one mushroom-shaped staddle stone to another were strong, rough-hewn beam; on top of them were criss-cross smaller timbers so that a kind of slatted floor stood about two feet six inches off the cobbled stone rickyard. Then came the faggots of withy wood and nut to fill the gaps in the staddle so that the sheaves were safe off the damp ground and safe from the rats, which could not climb the staddle stones because of the mushroom shape.

A littering of loose straw completed the staddle and then Nailus started the rick. He began building in the middle with a stook of six sheaves leaning against each other with the ears uppermost.

The first course were placed all around with the ears a little higher than the butt end.

Around the perimeter of the round rick, Nailus on his knees placed every sheaf with the butt end (or end which was cut from the stubble) neatly in line so that all that could be seen from the ground was the ends of the straw sheaves, the ears all turned to the centre of the rick.

Alf Rogers handed him the sheaves, or rather he pitched them to him, butt ends first with a short shuppick.

Bob Cuthbert came with Annette and Gwen in the pony and trap, bringing drinks and food for the men. And so the harvest of the corn went apace.

The Goldfield men were still very sore about losing what promised to be a bumper plum crop with the Spring frosts.

Then came the Harvest Festival where Rev Cuthbert explained how God moves in a mysterious way and that the year had not been an easy one for his flock.

But Mr Mathison and Mr Samson had helped the stricken folk of the Goldfields, as they had rescued Alf Rogers. Boots, Booker and Jack and Alf still looked glum.

"If only that one fateful night the blow had been spared!"

Every week at the Cider Mill the men of Netherstone paid their club money to a stranger who came to the village, a dealer in livestock, furniture.

"A'ligger," Nailus called him.

When the fruit, the few apples that escaped the frost, the flowers, the pumpkins had been cleared from the church and sent to Pershore Workhouse, another blow fell. The dealer had left the district and gone to Canada with the club money.

One hundred pounds Joe Badger said he had collected to be shared out at Christmas.

The news spread like wild fire. Boots, Booker, Hellfire Jack, Alf Rogers walked to Pershore and met the small holders there whose crop of plums had been meagre owing to the Spring frost.

After a few pints they sang this song.

> You ask me where and whence I come.
>   Pershore, God help us;
> Don't ask about the crops at home,
>   God help us;
> Last April, every sprig and spray
> Was deck'd with pearly blossoms gay,
> Last August, every branch and bough
> Was bent with yellow plums, but now,
>   God help us;
>
> Where do we cease in laugh to bend?
>   Pershore, God help us;

Why, one would think the world at end,
   God help us,
For every mortal in the place,
Doth seem to wear a fiddle face;
The Land of Plums so blest of late,
Seems dreary, nude and desolate,
   God help us;

Where is it Jill hath pawn'd her dress?
   Pershore, God help us;
And Jack's as bad as Bill or Bess,
   God help us;
Here's Giles the gardener in arrears,
And Black and Brown are both in tears,
And many more will come to pot,
Good Lord; the court will see the lot,
   God help us;

Where have we nought to make us wine?
   Pershore, God help us,
Why, that's enough to make us pine,
   God help us;
Last year we did the Highland fling,
But like the starved chapel mice,
We go with tears in our eyes,
   God help us.

Who last year held the Harvest home?
   Pershore, God help us;
The Lord knows when the next will come;
   God help us;
Of yore we piled the festive board,
The room with jest and laughter roar'd,
And want is in its place supplied;
   God help us.

Who last year loudly thank'd the Lord?
  Pershore, God help us;
And now we scarcely raise a word,
  God help us;
We know we still owe thanks, but then,
We cannot sing nor say amen,
But when to church we do repair,
We breathe this little humble pray'r
  God help us.

So winter came with the men of the Goldfields working part time on Mathison and Samson estate. How else could they buy bread and a bit of Canterbury lamb to Sunday's?

"'Tis very hard," Old Nailus told Mr Samson, "when a man struggles to climb the ladder starting with a few acres of land, then everything goes against him."

Tom Samson agreed and thought of the time when he started farming at Netherstone.

"One bit of good news I have for you, Nailus. Rev Cuthbert is paying the Club members out of his own pocket at Christmas."

Nailus blew his nose to hide a tear with his handkerchief as he replied:

"I allus knew as young Bob Cuthbert was a practical Christian."

On Christmas Eve Nailus knew that his work on the land would be over. The land he loved would no longer be trod by his hob-nailed boots.

Tom and Monty had decided that he should retire.

In the Netherstone School recently built by the Church, Mathison and Samson organized a Christmas Eve dinner.

After the plates had been cleared away, Annette played the piano, Gwen sang solos and duets with Wilf. The village bell ringers played pieces on their hand bells. The concert was impromptu in a very real sense.

The sight which touched the villagers most of all was the

Vicar and his old Aunt sitting at the school mistress's desk handing out the Club money to all the members.

The calamity of the Spring frost was spoken of by him as he said that the little he had done in recompensing the Club was quite small compared with the way the farmers of Netherstone farms had found employment for the men of the Goldfields.

Then came quite unexpectedly the highlight of the evening. Aaron Hicks had sung the 'Farmer's Boy' with his usual gusto, when Squire Monty Mathison spoke from the top table.

"It's a little sad here tonight for Tom Samson and myself to part with one of our most faithful men, Nailus Bullin, but part we must. Nailus has ploughed his last furrow, but I would be glad if he could come forward."

A tall, bent, angular man with a walking stick stood up from his chair.

It was Nailus in a tidy tweed coat, cord waistcoat and corduroy trousers. He walked up the aisle between the chairs. As he walked the corduroy of his trousers smelt new from the tailor, and his knees rubbed together making a noise like the intermittent note of a turtle dove as cord rubbed against cord. He stood bareheaded and wrinkled before his employers. The Squire handed him a leather purse containing five golden sovereigns, Tom Samson gave him a card, Kate was called up to stand with him in front of the table and Tom Samson asked her to read the words written in gold.

This certificate is in appreciation of the loyal service and hard work by Nailus Bullin on Netherstone Farms for fifty years and we Montague Mathison and Thomas Samson agree to pay him ten shillings a week as long as he lives and grant him his cottage free of all rent; signed

Montague Mathison and Thomas Samson.

As Kate put her arms around the old carter, Netherstone men and women stood up and clapped.

"Thank you kindly, gentlemen," Nailus said. "I cannot say any more at present," and the old couple walked back to their seats.

A new era had begun at Netherstone when the hiss of steam became more common on the land, and the good and faithful old labourer Nailus had played his part.

ALSO BY FRED ARCHER

AND AVAILABLE IN CORONET

All these books are available at your local bookshop or newsagent, or can be ordered direct from the publisher. Just tick the titles you want and fill in the form below.

Prices and availability subject to change without notice.

....

CORONET BOOKS, P.O. Box 11, Falmouth, Cornwall.

Please send cheque or postal order, and allow the following for postage and packing:

U.K. – One book 18p plus 8p per copy for each additional book ordered, up to a maximum of 66p.

B.F.P.O. and EIRE – 18p for the first book plus 8p per copy for the next 6 books, thereafter 3p per book.

OTHER OVERSEAS CUSTOMERS – 20p for the first book and 10p per copy for each additional book.

Name..

Address ....

....